THAT KIND OF GUY

Mina V. Esguerra

This book is a work of fiction. Names, characters, places, and incidents are products of the author's imagination or are used fictitiously. Any resemblance to actual events or locales or persons, living or dead, is entirely coincidental.

First published in 2012

Cover designed by Tania Arpa
Photography by Alexandra Urrea

Prologue

This time, the story came from someone named Rikki Taruc. She was easily five inches taller than me, and the way her hair fell down her back couldn't possibly be natural.

"It was my first time at that branch," she said, referring to the gym chain she usually went to. "It just happened that I had a meeting in Shangri-La that day, and the yoga sked was perfect. I didn't know anybody so I stayed in the back row, and then this guy came up beside me."

She noticed him right away, taking in all she could from between downward dogs and adjusting her warrior pose. The attraction—at least on her part—was instant. She fidgeted with her ponytail, self-consciously checked if her anti-perspirant was working, struggled to keep that look of peaceful concentration on her face for as long as the class was going.

Then they had to partner up to assist each other with headstands, and a shiver went down her spine when he looked her way and gestured toward the wall.

She liked the way he lifted her up: like he was sure of himself, like she could lean her entire weight on his hands. Whatever meditative purpose this was supposed to serve was lost on her completely. And then when it was his turn, he didn't need her at all. He lifted his own legs up, assured (though not necessarily graceful), and brought himself back upright like nothing had happened.

"I'm Rikki," she said, when everyone started packing up.

"Anton Santos," he answered.

After her meeting they had dinner, and then saw each other again three other times. Within a week and a half.

"And that was it?" I asked.

Rikki smiled. "Yeah, that was it."

"When was this?"

"Four years ago, August." She didn't even need to think about it. "I know it well because it was right after my boyfriend broke up with me. Then when he found out what happened with Anton, he was like, *We're never getting back together* and I was like, *So what, jerk?*"

"How did you two break it off?" I asked. "You and Anton, I mean."

Rikki shrugged, lifting a hand, and that was when I noticed the perfectly shaped fingernails with intricate nail art on each one. "Break it off? It's not like that. I mean, I thought it was fairly obvious the last time I saw him. I went to his place, and didn't feel the need to stay the night. Not like he wanted me to either. It felt like that was it."

"No drama?"

"Oh there was drama when my mother found out what I had done, but I didn't involve him in that."

"Interesting," I said.

"How about you?" Rikki asked. "How did you end it?"

Rikki was not a friend, by the way. I hadn't even known her an hour ago. It happened that I was invited to a friend's house for her son's birthday, and they had introduced me to their accountant friend, Rikki. She said I looked familiar, and remembered that she had seen me in a photo with Antonio U. Santos. So I asked her how she knew him, and she told me.

"I said I didn't feel like being with a guy like him anymore," I said, letting the white wine swirl in the glass I was holding.

Rikki nodded, eyes big and full of empathy. "Oh I get what you mean. Anton is... relationships with him have an expiry date. You really have to get out before you get hurt."

I sighed. "Right."

"When were *you* with him?"

"Last year."

"How long were you together?"

Truth was, I never discussed my relationship with Anton that much. Even if other women offered up extraordinarily detailed stories, I shared just enough—to make them feel like we were similar, but hiding what might have made me different.

"Not long," I said, shrugging. "I don't remember even."

Rikki laughed, finishing off her wine. "Sister, I say move on and find a real man now, if you haven't already. We all know Anton is just a delicious distraction. He's like that dream that we all eventually wake up from."

"Cheers," I said, hoping it didn't sound hollow. Rikki at least wasn't the type of girl who followed Anton's life much after their time together, so being evasive was much easier.

She didn't know, for example, that we were together for eleven months. After nearly a decade of dating around, he had experimented with having a "serious girlfriend," and it didn't turn out as he had hoped. She also didn't know (because no one ever really did) that we broke up after he sincerely proposed marriage to me, and I said no.

***

That night, after meeting Rikki, I pulled out the notebook from its place at the bottom of my night table's middle shelf. Underneath the sanitary pads, which hopefully deterred prying eyes and hands. It was a small, nicely-bound notebook with non-ruled sheets that I had converted it into a calendar.

I riffled through the pages for August, four years ago, and wrote "Rikki Taruc, accountant, yoga class" on the corresponding page. There was already an entry there:

"Mika no last name, cocktail waitress/culinary arts student, friend's wedding."

Nobody knew about the notebook of hook-up stories, and I would never discuss it, even with my dearest friends. This was my secret shame of the past seven months, the exact amount of time since Anton and I had broken up. If during our entire relationship I willingly avoided any sordid stories about his past, now that we weren't together, I actually resorted to documenting them.

I wish one of my friends knew. Or maybe my sister. She would tell me how crazy this was.

Julie, you are crazy. Are these stories making you feel better about saying no?

Every day I had to remind myself that they did.

***

Annemarie, February, six years ago, didn't meet him by accident. She sought him out. The month before, her best friend Lani had gotten her into trouble by telling her boyfriend how many guys she had been with, and she got back at the goody-goody by looking for the one-night stand who never called Lani back.

She was surprised that her friend actually went for him—Lani usually liked lean with curly locks like a schoolboy teen star; not buff, slightly dangerous, shaved head. Because they had an odd friendship, she found it only natural to try her luck with the guy too, and he obliged.

"I still don't know why he didn't call her though," Annemarie admitted. "He never let me ask him about it."

"I think the pattern is, if the girl had too much fun he would never agree to see her again," I responded, strangely detached from my own voice.

"True," she said. "Lani was obsessed for weeks. She only really stopped when she found out that I slept with him. Helped her get over him. Weird how that turned out, right?"

"You still friends with her now?"

"Of course."

I met Annemarie at my office Christmas party. I worked at a small publishing company as a managing editor, and she was the date of one of the circulation managers. She, on the other hand, knew about me.

"I can't believe Anton actually had a girlfriend. Like, a real girlfriend. How long did it last? A year?"

I shrugged. "Not a year."

Lani (November, seven years ago) was in the notebook too.

These were the women who were attracted to my ex.

Chapter 1

I showed up for my first day of work in red, pointy shoes with four-inch heels. That was why my officemates hated me.

I wouldn't have done it if it weren't for my sister who brainwashed me the night before and told me that I should "show them who's boss."

That was two years ago, and I *did* kind of show them who the boss was. The problem was that I was apparently replacing someone they had loved working for, someone who wore jeans and sneakers, drank beer with them every Friday, and resigned "as a statement" when he found out that I was being brought in to be co-managing editor. My grand entrance, complete with smart dress suit and red, pointy shoes, made it so clear to the team which editor they preferred. Also, I didn't really like to drink beer.

These people made my place of work cold and unfriendly at best, hostile and hellish at worst. Monday mornings were a dreaded chore, like having to go to the dentist to have my teeth cleaned. Every week.

It wasn't like this when I was a teacher. I taught college-level English at my alma mater for a few years, while I took my master's degree. Sure, I got annoyed at my students sometimes, especially when they preferred to give their laptops the attention they should have given me, but it never got this bad. I never had to lie in bed wide awake, thinking of new but non-serious diseases to claim I had, so I could take sick leaves.

My younger, more gregarious, and apparently more thick-skinned sister deflected any blame I sent her way. "They hate you because they're incompetent and they don't like it when you point it out to them," Andrea said, more than once. "Don't you dare blame my shoes, Manang."

***

So that was how I lost my officemates. My friends, I lost one by one because of stuff I said.

I didn't really *lose* them forever, by the way. Maybe that was a bit dramatic. But over the years I became the kind of person who liked to tell people the harsh truth—that they were stupid for making *that* decision.

Technically I never fought with anyone, and if I happened to see them at the mall or elsewhere, we'd hug and genuinely say we missed each other. I noticed a pattern in some of my friends' lives—they'd tell stories of their latest romantic mishap at dinner, moan about it at the next one, claim to be over it by the third one, and then plunge into the exact same predicament the next time I saw them.

Sorry if I didn't find that entertaining. Was I the minority for actually feeling *sad* when a friend went through these things? I didn't feel like laughing and offering to buy a round of drinks when the nth girlfriend moaned about being treated badly and worrying about being lonely forever. That wasn't funny.

As someone who had never had a serious boyfriend, I kind of took that thing... *seriously*.

"Please don't go back to him. You know he's never going to change," I once said to a friend.

"Well, you'll never end up in a serious relationship with anyone if you keep escaping to other countries to supposedly 'find yourself,'" was another thing I said.

To another friend: "Be careful around her—I saw her nearly making out with some other guy in a restaurant. Does she think you'll be okay with that?"

So they stopped telling me about these little things. And they also stopped inviting me to "vent over drinks." People who were conflicted enough about their own mistakes didn't really like anyone else pointing it out. A lesson I learned eventually, along with "people who loved their previous boss will resent any move the new boss will make."

"You're such a *manang*, Manang," my sister told me. Andrea lived like my friends did, never mind if I kept calling her on it. She and I were built differently. She was four years younger but was way ahead of me in terms of guys dated, relationships had, and hearts broken. It pained me to see her get into these avoidable scrapes, and I kept telling her where exactly she was going wrong, but she never listened to me. She couldn't hide from me though, not the way my friends did. We still lived in the same house.

***

I was twenty-five years old but my sister had been calling me "Manang" since we were kids. That was probably the reason why I met Antonio U. Santos at all.

The word actually means "older woman" but every group of friends has one, I think, even if they're all the same age. Andrea was not the first and only person to call me that. Some friends did too, and it's often been a term of endearment.

On behalf of the *manangs* of the world, I would like to say that we usually have the best intentions. I didn't particularly enjoy making someone feel bad, or raining on someone's parade.

I was also, for the most part, a nice girl. Not someone who was drawn to the wrong kind of guy, or who would end up having a hook-up story to tell at a random party. Or was it because I was never given the chance before? One day, someone took it upon herself to "loosen me up" and introduce me to a "fun guy," and of course, that was when things turned around.

Chapter 2

My first date with Anton was a casual thing. I was given his number, I gave him a call, he agreed to meet me at a restaurant after work. It didn't last very long; it really was just dinner. I think I ordered chicken curry. (What a mistake.) At one point, he said I had a bit of basil stuck in my teeth and I rushed to the bathroom to remove it.

The standout memories from that night were that: he was hot, and that I felt horribly underdressed in my black jeans and what used to be my best office top. Not that he did anything to make me feel insecure. If he thought my outfit was inappropriate, he never let that on. Instead he flashed his smile at me, in much the way the other girls described, and asked the proper questions one asked on a first date. Maybe it was during this conversation that I found out he worked as a financial analyst at one of the larger firms in the country. And that he was thirty years old, and single.

I didn't *meet* hot guys. I knew some good-looking ones, but they were never really into me, or available for me to date. This guy was *there*, and my date. It was unsettling.

My idea of small talk was to tell him that I was twenty-five and stuck. I told him about the hater drama at work, because at the time that was all I ever talked about.

"What do you mean, haters?" Anton asked, relaxing into his chair. At this point, his shoe lightly brushed the tip of mine under the table, and I shivered a tiny bit. I wished I weren't so transparent. "What exactly do they do to you?"

How did they hate me? *Let me count the ways.* "I'm never invited to their get-togethers. Or birthday *merienda* at four PM, even if they're having *pancit* and cake right there at a workstation beside me. There's apparently an office tradition when someone new joins the team—

everyone pitches in for a card and a dinner, and I never got that. When I ask for anything, I always get it five minutes after my deadline. When something goes wrong, they find a way to blame me for it—and it's never to my face, because I'm not copied in those emails. I only find out because my boss actually *likes* me, and lets me know when someone on my team goes behind my back and says stuff about me."

I may have said more. I probably talked about that, monologue-like, for a huge chunk of time.

Afterward, Anton laughed, and it was charming. Not at all like he was patronizing me. "And you're the boss, right?"

"In theory, yes."

"Then fire the idiots."

My eyes nearly popped out of my head, which he found as amusing. "But I can't."

"Of course you can. They'll learn their lesson quick that way."

"No, I mean I know that... but I can't. I don't have the authority to do that... and my career hasn't been affected by this. Firing anyone is a bit extreme."

"Thing is, they work *for* you. They shouldn't be giving you this kind of trouble."

"They'll shape up eventually. Everybody needs a job."

He paused and gave me a strange look. "You're a modern saint."

I wasn't sure how I went from venting about my hateful co-workers to defending their right to employment, but I didn't say anything untrue. Even with the crappy treatment, it never occurred to me to fire anyone, like I had unconsciously drawn that line. That little conversation made me admit it. I cleared my throat and returned his look, not really knowing what to say.

That could have been a moment between us, but suddenly someone tapped him on the shoulder and said hi. It was a friend who happened to be in the same restaurant. By the time I finished my curry, three more friends had done the same thing, and we settled back into safe, shallow topics like favorite vacation spots (Him: Boracay and Dumaguete; Me: Palawan) and concerts recently seen (Him: some DJ and some indie band I'd never heard of; Me: A friend's band, but it didn't count).

Our first date ended at the curb in front of the restaurant. I had insisted on getting a cab—I didn't want to join him to his next stop, a party at a friend's house, and suspected he was being polite when he invited me. I said I was sleepy, and that I felt a cold coming on, and three other lame excuses. He politely bent to brush our cheeks together. Was it a polite *beso* or a kiss-off? I sided with the latter. That was probably the lamest first date anyone had ever had with Anton.

Chapter 3

The second date was worse, if that was even possible.

Dinner was at an Italian restaurant owned by one of Anton's friends. I didn't mind that he took the lead on the choice again, because I'd heard good things about the place anyway and wanted to try it. It was also a quick walk from work, and I knew the neighborhood well enough to make a quick getaway if I needed to.

Halfway through probably the best ravioli I'd ever had, I saw something across the room that bothered me. I saw the girl that one of my closest friends was dating, and she was with another guy.

It was definitely her. I wasn't imagining it, and when her dinner companion kind of nuzzled her neck, it became clear to me that it wasn't a casual meal.

Now see, this was the kind of thing I never wanted to see or find out, because I knew exactly what I was going to do. And people never liked it. Anton kept taking trips from our table to speak to his friend, and other friends, so I had time to slip out and give her a piece of my mind.

Eventually, despite being away from our table half the time, Anton noticed that I seemed preoccupied.

"Is the pasta that bad? Because we can have them do it again," he offered, half joking.

"No, it's all right," I said. "It's really good."

"More wine?"

"No," I said quickly, knowing that he'd probably be away for five minutes again once I asked for a refill. "I needed to get something off my chest. And now I have. I should be okay."

"I'm sorry. Are you sick? Should I get you something, like for a headache?"

I wished he would stay put. But I wasn't in the mood to be charming. "If you found out that your friend's girlfriend was cheating on him, what would you do?"

That got him to sit down. "I wouldn't say anything."

"What if your friend finds out anyway and gets mad at you for not saying anything?"

"I usually let my friends make their own mistakes. I get to sit back and laugh."

"I'm not kidding," I said. "Because I'm the type who would say something. I would tell him about her, so he doesn't stay in the dark about something this important to him."

"I'm assuming this has happened before?"

"Kind of. Not necessarily the cheating, but the saying something that someone doesn't want to hear, yes."

A waiter refilled our glasses of water without needing Anton's intervention, which was apparently possible, and for that I was glad. He barely noticed the waiter as he searched my face, probably realizing that I was taking this seriously. "So you don't think that kind of information is none of your business, and that two people in a relationship should figure out their issues themselves?"

I shook my head. "My loyalty is to my friend. If I know something, I'll say it."

"Have you ever been in a relationship?"

My heart sped up, defensive. "No."

"Interesting. Because couples tend to know they're in trouble even before someone tells them, you know? If you leave them alone long enough, things will happen according to nature—"

"I don't believe that," I said. "Then how do you explain how people get blindsided when their relationship ends? Because that happens. A lot."

He shrugged. "They willingly live in denial. You can't really keep a secret if you're as close as you're supposed to be, in a relationship."

"I've heard that you haven't been in one for a while," I said.

"Maybe I don't want anyone messing with my secrets."

"Ugh. This fear of commitment by a twenty-something male is so cliche. I'm not even talking about relationships—I asked you about how you would show your loyalty to a friend. On principle I would tell him if I knew anything that would affect his relationship, because I don't want anyone lying to my friend."

"I'm thirty," Anton reminded me, unfazed. "And look—I don't mean to say you're wrong. I'd actually like to have you watching out for me, if this is how you are. I'm saying I'd probably mind my own business."

Instead of responding, I angrily gulped down my water. At the time, I pretty much ruled out any future with this guy. How could we last, when we disagreed on something as fundamental to me as this? But whatever, I probably wasn't meant for Anton anyway.

Later, he confessed that this was when he started to like me. So what do I know about anything?

Chapter 4

He kept calling me. At the time, I didn't know why.

We went out two more times, and each time felt like that first date all over again. Our conversations were *fine*, and I was starting to get comfortable around him, but something was interrupting whatever mood I could have been in.

"You okay?" Anton liked to ask, tapping my glass. I learned that he meant a refill, and whenever I said yes, he wouldn't just call the waiter. He would *get up* and head to the bar himself, like he was entertaining me in his own place. Anton got away with this because he was a regular at every place he brought me to, and the owners and staff all knew him by name.

This meant that every time he left the table, I got to tap my feet and check out the interior décor, while he chatted with the inevitable friend he was "surprised" to bump into. These friends, I would learn once he got back to me, could not be ignored—they were models, actors, athletes, business people... I recognized their last names even if I had never seen their faces before.

When he eventually returned to me, I'd be deep in thought about something. "What are you thinking?" he would say, as if he wanted to be included in the conversation I was having with myself.

"Your crowd is a bit more high-profile than mine," was one of my answers.

"You think? Nobody recognizes most of them." He said this to make me feel better, but it wasn't as convincing as he thought it would be.

"When *my* friends and I get recognized, it's probably because we're somewhere college kids hang out." My "crowd" was mostly made up of teachers, and yeah, we got recognized a lot because we could only afford to hang out where students did. Not that this was the same thing.

For three more dates this went on, each of them ending with a *beso* by the curb right before I got into my cab. On the way home that last time, still touching the cheek his lips had brushed gently, I finally admitted it: This wasn't fun.

Sure, Anton seemed like the happening guy, and he had all these happening friends. I spent four dinners always on the verge of getting to know someone interesting, and maybe he would prove to be that, if he didn't act like such a social butterfly half the time.

The next time he called and asked me out again—why did he even keep doing that—I said I was busy.

***

"Every day? You're kidding."

"Of course." Good thing he couldn't see me over the phone because my face was scrunched up the awkward way it does when I lie.

He paused and the sound of techno-type music filled the silence. And then, "I'll go with you."

"What? When?"

"Tomorrow. What time is it again?"

"You're kidding. It's too early."

"What time is it?"

I coughed. "Four AM."

"Not a problem. My night would just be ending. I'll see you, we'll have breakfast, and then I'll go off to bed. That fine?"

Why didn't he stop calling me? Not being available half a dozen times wasn't enough of a hint? So I finally said I couldn't possibly go out with him that night, because I had *Simbang Gabi* super early the next day.

Only because I thought that an early morning Catholic mass was the last thing he'd want to mess with.

"Fine, see you there," I said weakly.

I immediately felt that I had to apologize to my great-grandmother. *Lola, it's not a lie if I actually do go tomorrow. I didn't just use* Simbang Gabi *as an excuse. I will actually go.*

My great-grandmother on my mother's side made sure that I attended every single day of the nine-day service that led up to Christmas. She passed away when I was ten, and with her went any obligation for me to wake up for the early morning mass.

Oh well, maybe she would be happy that I was going again.

A few hours later, I was up at a crazy early hour and ready to meet Anton in church. It was true, he looked like he was at the end of a really long day, and I still had no idea what he was doing there.

"I had an extra espresso right before I got here to make sure I don't fall asleep on you," he said proudly, and a little too cheerfully.

"You didn't have to... you're probably so tired by now."

He shrugged like it was nothing, like he attended early morning mass all the time. "I am, but it doesn't matter. Whatever you have time for."

After mass, we had a quick *bibingka* breakfast at the cafeteria next door, and I sent him home to sleep as the caffeine started to wear off. He quickly kissed my cheek and said, "Same time tomorrow, right?"

***

On the third day of *Simbang Gabi* he sent me a message: *Need to be at work early for a call tomorrow, won't be able to join you for mass.*

"Thank God," I said and with another apology to my *lola,* skipped that mass entirely and got a good night's sleep.

That night he texted me again: *See you at four?*

So the next day, I went through the motions, and again woke up for mass bright and early. He was waiting for me, looking more refreshed than usual, and didn't strike up a conversation until mass had ended and we were back out on the street.

Then, he said: "You're a fake."

"What?"

"Faker." Anton looked entirely pleased with himself.

"What are you talking about?"

"I was *here* yesterday. My morning call was cancelled but I didn't tell you, thought I'd surprise you here at church. But you weren't here. So tell me, pious Julie Crisostomo, do you really go to *Simbang Gabi* every day? Or is this all part of a 'modern saint' act that I'm supposed to like?"

Shit shit shit.

It was too early and I was too sleepy, and I was a horrible liar. Seconds passed and I had nothing to say in defense of myself.

"What are you thinking?" he said.

All I could do was let out a little shriek and I instinctively grabbed his arm.

"You weren't supposed to come!" I admitted, with much relief. "I only said I had to go to mass every day because I thought it would get you to *stop* calling me, but you keep showing up!"

"Why do you want to get rid of me?"

"Do you really think this is working out?" I was exasperated. "It's been weeks and we barely know each other. And your scene isn't really mine, and I doubt that you'd really want to do what I want to do... I don't know. I thought it was obvious."

It felt good to say that, to be honest, because Anton could be remarkably resilient when it came to the truth. He let it slide. "Well how do we know that for sure when you've been faking?"

"I haven't been—"

"Yes you have."

I shook my head and started laughing. "Fine. Maybe a little."

"Okay, I'm sorry that our dates haven't been your thing, but you should have said something. If you're going to reject me, reject me because of something *real*, not some rule you invented that you didn't tell me about."

"All right then."

"Ask me out this weekend and make sure we do something *you* want to do."

"Fine."

"And then you can find a good reason to reject me."

"Why do you keep asking me out?"

He smiled. "I think you're going to be good for me. And I do want someone like you watching out for me. Is that wrong?"

It wasn't. Right then he kissed me, on the mouth, for the first time. It felt like a challenge, unlike anything I'd been asked to do in the short time that I'd been dating.

I agreed, but sincerely thought it wouldn't last. I really did believe that he would find me boring and eventually leave me.

Chapter 5

It wasn't just the *manang* thing, or that I was mostly unadventurous by nature. I never moved out of my parents' house because... well, there was no reason, really. I just didn't do it. I happened to like the company of my dad, who worked all his life in car dealerships, and my mom, a serial entrepreneur. Once Andrea and I stopped the childhood sisterly fighting, she was nicer to have around too.

If this kind of life influenced my relationships, I couldn't be sure. I knew that as a given, any guy I liked had to be cool with my family. My parents met all of my friends, and took pics of me with my prom dates. They weren't strict when it came to guys and they never commented explicitly on them, but on date nights, my parents (early sleepers, usually) were always mysteriously up late, watching TV in the living room.

The first time Anton and my dad met, they bonded over cars, a passion his two daughters didn't have. I hadn't seen my dad light up like that in a conversation with a near-stranger. My mom was more hesitant at first, after seeing Anton and noticing that he was a bit too smooth. She told me to be careful, that I was genetically programmed to like a "bad boy."

I said, "But Dad isn't like that at all."

And she said, "You didn't know him back then. Oh my God."

Ew, Mom.

Eventually, Anton got the seal of my mom's approval—a standing invitation to Sunday lunch. He showed up every two weeks or so, always with dessert or a bottled delicacy that my mom fawned over.

***

After a month, I ran out of places I wanted us to have dinner at.

Anton took my suggestions seriously. Even when they seemed so pedestrian, he was a good sport and took me there. He went along with my food ideas, too, and eventually started to share dishes with me. I discovered that the guy could eat anything—he was not allergic, not picky, and very opinionated but polite about it. He was indifferent toward the baked lasagna I loved at a restaurant in TriNoMa, but ordered seconds at the *sisig* place near my old high school.

"I see a pattern," he said, after several dinner dates. "Comfort food."

I shrugged. "That's not a pattern. All food is comfort food to me."

"The way you choose your meals. Have you ever chosen anything recently that you haven't tried before?"

"That's not *fair,*" I said. "I'm showing you my favorite places. Of course I'll order the stuff I like so you can try them."

Anton leaned back in his chair, still sold on his own analysis. "You know I'd try whatever you get for me. But you never choose something new for yourself."

I rolled my eyes. "You're putting too much meaning into this."

"Do you know that you look so uncomfortable when scrutinized? It's cute."

"Then *stop doing it.*"

My ideas for date restaurants ran out on a Sunday, just after we'd digested the mango torte he brought as an offering to my mom, and as we were planning where to have dinner. We were establishing a new routine, and while I felt prickly and awkward at each turn, he took everything in stride. At this point, for example, I didn't even call him my boyfriend yet. He was the guy who took me out to dinner, and came over on Sundays with cake. He also hung out all afternoon in the family room, talking to my dad, reading my dad's car magazines. I offered more than once to go out somewhere, in case he wanted to be saved from small talk with my parents, but he never took me up on it. Eventually everyone, myself included, got used to him being there, doing nothing.

Before I met him, I wondered how I could possibly fit a relationship into my life. My days felt full, of people, things, and concerns, and I wondered what I'd have to give up to accommodate someone new. Anton made it seem easy. He didn't take me *out* of my life; instead, he sort of slid into the empty spaces and made himself comfortable.

"You feel like Italian food?" I asked, kicking off my slippers and stretching my legs on the sofa. He was sitting at the other end, flipping through the car magazine he had picked up last time but hadn't finished.

Anton shrugged. "I don't know," he said, sleepily. "I had pasta yesterday." He caught one of my ankles, nonchalantly, nothing to it, and absently drummed his fingertips on it.

I coughed and resisted the tickle impulse. "Chinese?"

"Like dimsum?"

I shook my head. "Not in the mood for dimsum. I wonder if I'd like Japanese."

"My friend opened a ramen place in Quezon City, if you want to try it."

I gently kicked his side. "Maybe."

He laughed. "Right, right, I remember. New places."

"I'm stuck," I admitted. "I can't think of a place we haven't tried yet."

"That's all you've got? Millions of people live in Metro Manila. They're all eating *somewhere.*"

I let him rib me on that for a bit more, and then he came up with this—we should go out and try something new. As we walked side by side to the driveway where his car was parked (he only had a car when we went out on weekends, I noticed) he asked, "Where do we go? Name a street."

"I can't think of any."

And then he gave me that look. It was his thing. He didn't like it when I was being indecisive, and sometime between dinner number four and five, he found a way to get me to quickly make a decision. Anton lifted my wrist and tickled me underneath my rib cage. "I *said*, name a street. Anywhere in Makati."

"Jupiter!" I yelled, trying to leap out of his grasp.

So we drove the length of Jupiter Street, then decided on a restaurant neither of us had tried. It was a small vegetarian place near the end of the stretch. He had the tofu burger, I had mushroom pasta, and we both thought it was a good call. He was so impressed that he asked for information about the chef and the owner, if they had other branches anywhere, if they delivered, if they catered. In no time at all, he had was on first-name basis with the manager, forty-two-year-old Alice, and had made a new friend.

"He's charming," Alice said to me, when Anton excused himself to go to the bathroom. "How long have you been together?"

That might have been the first time a stranger assumed we were together. "Not long," I said.

"Are you into vegetarian food too?"

She seemed genuinely interested in *me*, and what I had to say. I did my best to be even half as charming as my date was. He eventually came back to the table, Alice left us alone, and I felt even though this had started out as neutral territory, he had made it his. I guess I couldn't totally take that out of him. But it didn't bother me as much, maybe because *we* had discovered the place together.

That seemed like a nice story to tell.

Chapter 6

The only other person who really saw the relationship progress was Andrea.

It may have been sometime during the third month of my exclusively dating Anton when Andrea showed up in my room and flopped onto my bed next to me.

"So is Anton your boyfriend already?" she asked.

I hadn't used that word for him yet—not to his face, or anyone else. "Maybe?"

"Where have you let him touch you?"

"Ugh, I won't even answer that."

"Oh please. I tell *you* everything!"

"Because you don't have manners or respect for your boytoys."

Andrea smiled and kind of pulled at my earlobe. "I'll wait. You'll tell me anyway, because you won't be able to help it. You'll want to ask me if certain things are normal or not."

"Is that why you keep telling *me* these things?"

"Who else? Not Mom. And you're here all the time, Manang," Andrea said that so matter-of-factly, I wasn't sure whether to be flattered or offended. "I'm kind of surprised that you'd bring home a guy like him, though."

"What does that mean?"

"Don't get me wrong. I know you and from what you've told me about him... it's the *bagay* thing."

When we were younger, Andrea and I used to play this game while we were in restaurants and other public spaces. We would watch as couples walked by, and instantly judge if they were "*bagay*." Right for each other. It was a futile but entertaining exercise, especially when girls who hadn't experienced love were doing it, because inevitably we judged on appearances. If a couple looked *bagay*, or right for each other, I would know it on sight. But it wasn't a consistent thing. Over the years that we played this game, we got to see the many possible combinations. Yet I never got to articulate why I thought a couple *looked right* together.

If I had to guess, I'd say it wasn't how they looked at all, but the way they were around each other.

Andrea, on the other hand, went by a totally different gut reaction, but she had a good eye for these things too so I couldn't say that she was *wrong*.

"You don't think we're right for each other?" I demanded.

She squinted thoughtfully, like she was evaluating something right in front of her. "I wouldn't *say that*. It's... unexpected. Not the kind of guy I thought you'd introduce to the parents."

"Because he's way out of my league?"

"I thought you'd be attracted to the slightly pudgy lit geek type. Like the guys who liked you in college."

I shrugged. "Remember, I never had a boyfriend in college."

"Yeah, but at least you know their kind. Do you know Anton's kind?"

***

Thing was, Anton knew early on that I wasn't comfortable with his partying friends and partying lifestyle. So he kept me out of it. He would talk about them sometimes, but only if I asked.

He called on a Thursday evening, after work, while I was walking to the nearest underpass. "*Quezo de bola ensaymadas*. Was thinking of passing by the weekend market for them. Would your mom like that?"

"Yes," I said. "So they should expect you again on Sunday?"

"Yeah. How's your weekend? Anywhere you want to go?"

Deep breath. "Are your friends doing anything interesting?"

There was a pause. Then, tentatively, "Well yeah. Charlie and Kat have a dinner party they're invited to. Hosts bore them to death, and they asked if you and I could come along and keep them company."

"When is this?"

"Tomorrow night."

"Let's go."

"Really?"

"Yeah. I mean, it's been months. We haven't hung out with any of your friends at all."

Another pause. "Charlie and Kat are different anyway. You'd probably like them more than anyone else I know."

"Cool. Tell them we're game for tomorrow."

"Sure about that?" Maybe I wasn't convincing enough, because he sounded as tentative. "What are you thinking?"

We don't hang out with his friends because of me. Because I don't think I'll like them very much.

I felt a little bit scared, but I couldn't back out now. "Yes."

Chapter 7

Anton, though still a not-boyfriend, had already met my sister, parents, and half my clan when my mom invited him to a post-Christmas lunch. He immediately stood out like a sore thumb, smartly-dressed and clean and imposing, but people warmed up to him anyway. It was like they *wanted* to like him, wanted to find something about him they could connect with. With my dad, it was cars. With my grandfather, it was the fact that Anton was willing to listen to World War II stories and claimed to be a bit of a World War II nut—and actually mentioning books he owned to back it up.

It was the first time I had ever brought a guy to a family reunion. In the past, my grandmother would sit beside me and, after sizing up Andrea's latest boyfriend, say, "Don't worry about it. Some girls aren't *ligawin*."

Meaning, girls like Andrea (for whatever reason) always had some guy following them around. And other girls, like me, did not. All the guys who had *ever* asked me out had started out as my friends first and had usually known me for months. Or years.

"Yeah, I grow on people," I would say, or something to that effect.

Anton, I could see, was not the type who "grew" on anybody. His effect on a room, on a person, was immediate. It could go either way; someone would shake his hand, smile brightly and keep talking, or wince and find an excuse to leave.

He was surprised when I mentioned this to him.

"It wasn't like that before," he said. "I think I had to be introduced three times to a person before they even noticed me."

"It's different now. I think they already know your name even before they shake your hand."

Anton smirked. "Would you look at that? And it only took me ten years of crushing gym workouts. So easy."

***

Anton's friend Charlie happened to be better known as "Apollo Ortiz," only the most popular actor on TV. He rose to fame on a TV show that I never watched, found more fame when his career dipped and was rumored to be doing drugs, and rebounded by cleaning himself up and getting a new show and a hit romantic comedy movie. Not that I watched those either, but I knew him well enough from the seventeen or so billboards that had his face plastered on them.

Also, Anton's friend Kat, Charlie's apparent girlfriend, wasn't too shabby herself. She was an accomplished television writer and had in fact headed the writing team for the show that made Apollo/Charlie popular—as well as this new one that had saved his career. She didn't look familiar to me, but she had the same easy confidence about her, like I *should* know who she was.

We arrived all together at the dinner party in Forbes. Charlie driving his black SUV, Kat in front, Anton and I in the back. I was the last to be picked up, and all three gave my parents the courtesy of saying hello. My sister, uncharacteristically home that night, blushed deep red at seeing Apollo Ortiz in her living room, but got over the need to change out of her ratty shorts to have a picture taken with him.

When we were back outside, on the way to the car, Kat hugged me like we were old friends. "It's so great to finally meet you, Julie. We've heard stories. Not sure if they were all true."

She was welcoming and warm and all, but at that moment I wished I had worn something fancier than cologne, and maybe lipstick a deeper shade of red, and something not as boring as jeans and a top with puffy sleeves. Kat was older by a few years but I felt like I was... her teacher.

On the drive over, we got the background on this dinner party. British security specialist Mickey and Filipina interior designer Margo were not strictly Anton's friends. Margo was a distant cousin or aunt of Kat's, and she liked throwing dinner parties in her large, expensive home. Kat didn't like them but suffered through the pleasantries because of old obligations to Margo's family that pre-dated us all, and had invited me and Anton along to keep her from interacting with the hosts.

"She's okay with you bringing strangers, right?" I had to ask. I'd never gate crashed a fancy dinner party before.

"It's fine," Kat said. "Margo likes meeting young people. Keeps her young, she says."

"Botox is what's keeping her young," Charlie said.

"You have to remember to *shut up*," Kat scolded playfully. "Just smile. Like on your newest billboard." To me, she said, "Margo and Mickey, they always serve great food. You won't regret that, at least."

"Is this your first time at Mickey and Margo's party too?" I asked Anton.

"Yeah," he said, casually taking my hand in his. "It's our thing. We try stuff for the first time together," he said to his friends.

Kat and Charlie snickered their own way at the same time.

"Awww," Kat said.

"Dude, you're on something," Charlie said.

Anton caught my eye and kissed my hand. "Ignore the jaded people in this car. They've been with the same person for ten years and don't know what it's like to be young and in love anymore."

That launched another round of snark from his friends. I smiled and shrugged a silent, "*They just don't understand.*"

***

Couldn't help it. On the way up to the house, I caught my reflection on the SUV's dark tinted window and reapplied some lip gloss. "What?" Anton asked, watching me.

"My lips feel naked," I explained.

He promptly placed his mouth upon mine and kissed off most of the waxy balm. "No, they feel like candles. Put that away. You look fine."

Kat was right; Mickey and Margo were a little *too* happy to welcome us to their party. We were ushered right away on a quick tour of their home, decorated by Margo herself, and I made sure to compliment her and nod as if I understood art and all. Frankly, it all seemed a bit overdone. Fluted glass of white wine in hand, she showed us nearly every room of her home. I estimated that I could fit four houses the exact size as mine into the same space. It seemed more... cramped in here because of all the *art*.

Anton kept his poker face on during the whole parade of ostentation, but I could tell that he was trying to keep from laughing. His eyes kind of lit up, even though his mouth didn't move. One time he actually hid behind me, pressed his face against the back of my head, and shook as he let a hint of a laugh escape.

Our tour was cut short, thankfully, because someone alerted Margo that the food was ready.

"I'm *so* very sorry," she said, boozily pinching Anton's bicep out of nowhere. "I need to leave you for a second, but please make your way to the dining room as soon as you can."

As soon as she was out of earshot, I let myself smile. "It's not just Botox," I whispered.

"Are you kidding?" He absently touched the same spot she had. "There might be blood drinking involved."

"I will check every glass she hands you," I offered.

"I've met women like her before," he said offhandedly. "But thanks for watching my back."

Sure you have, I suddenly thought, remembering that he wasn't exactly new at this. I pushed that thought down, down, down and buried it under some really good French food.

Chapter 8

Things at work did not get better, but having something to look forward to every day did wonders for my mood. My officemates needed to be *extra* annoying to get me to react. The usual cold shoulder, casual disrespect, and deliberate disregard for my deadlines—*meh*, nothing. One time, when a staff writer submitted something ten minutes *after* my cutoff without explanation or apology, I found myself replying "Thanks!" (with exclamation point).

And then I sent another email to all writers announcing that "Daily deadline has now been moved an hour earlier, to 3 PM :)" (with smiley face).

My blood pressure did not spike; I was calm the whole time. I followed Anton's advice for a change—if they insisted on not respecting my authority, then I should assert it and remind them who was in charge.

But things did not go away. My escalation led to, apparently, a mini revolution, and in two weeks, I was called into the boss's office.

I liked my boss Christy. Australian, frizzy haired, and always looking like she was happy to see me. I found her easy to work with and a great mentor. The team resentment probably had a little to do with it. More of them wanted to be in a position where they'd be mentored by Christy, but I was in the way.

"I was in an interesting meeting yesterday," she said.

"Yes?" That was a weird intro. I braced myself for bad news.

"Some of the writers came to me, objecting to your new earlier deadline, and have told me that you've made the environment too stressful for them to produce quality work. Three of them have hinted that they would quit if I let this earlier deadline stand."

I began to hear my heartbeat. Like, in my ear. "What did you tell them?"

Christy cleared her throat and spoke with a measured tone. "I told them that if they routinely submit a story ten minutes *after* the four PM deadline then that's ten minutes longer the editors and web team have to stay to process the work before it can go up. Fact is, more people in this office would be happier if the writers submitted their work earlier. The three PM deadline stays."

I gulped. "Thank you."

"It was the right thing to do, Julie, but you have to learn how to deal with them. Part of your job is to make sure these... *things* are settled before I even hear about them."

"I understand," I said. "I'll be more assertive next time."

When I got back to my desk, I felt a prickly sensation in my nose, and mouth, and chest, and down my arms, and when I balled my right hand into a fist I had difficulty opening it again.

With my good hand, I fumbled for my phone and called Anton.

"I need you to pick me up," I said, trying to stay calm. "Now. You have to take me home."

Anton's office was a ten-minute walk from my building. "Are you okay? What happened?"

"I'm sick," I said, between short breaths. "Please come and get me."

We had a nurse and small clinic in the office but I didn't want anyone to see the effect their little stunt had on me. Instead, I quickly grabbed my things, parked myself on a couch by the reception desk, and waited for Anton, right fist still balled up beside me.

The receptionist looked concerned. "Are you sure you don't want to drop by the clinic first?"

"I'm sure," I said, still huffing and puffing. "My boyfriend's picking me up."

***

"So what happened?"

I wondered how far back I should go, but I had just gotten my breath and the use of my fist back. "I think those jerks tried to get me fired. By threatening to quit because of something I did."

"Did it work?"

"No."

"Are you sure you want to stay in this job?" He touched my forehead, like he was checking my temperature, and he looked concerned.

"I hate them, but I'm not quitting."

"You're too nice."

"I won't be after this."

He shrugged. "You handle it your way, but I'm not going to ask you to talk about this anymore."

The last time I had an episode like this was in grade six. I didn't remember much of what happened, only that it was really hot that day, and suddenly I felt like I couldn't breathe. Or that each breath I took wasn't enough. The school nurse calmed me down and said I didn't have to go to the ER, but suggested that I be taken home where it wasn't so hot and crowded.

I didn't have asthma, and hadn't felt anything like that since. Until now. The ride home was familiar but a little off, because this time, instead of my parents, it was my boyfriend who came by to pick me up and drive me home.

He found a bag I could breathe into, and I spent most of the ride trying to get my lungs back in shape. At home, he hovered around me the rest of the afternoon, and didn't bring up work until he felt I was ready to talk.

My boyfriend.

Chapter 9

I was Anton's girlfriend. I needed to get used to the idea.

Like with most aspects of this relationship, he let me set the pace, and only started acknowledging this official status once I had. It wasn't easy though. I had the weird feeling that I had *responsibilities*, being, you know, this guy's first serious girlfriend in years.

To start, I relented and we started seeing more of his friends. I owed him that, I thought, and it wasn't fair that he kept adjusting for me. I figured that I should at least make an effort. I hoped I'd get comfortable with those people eventually.

Apart from Sunday lunch with my family, Sunday dinner somewhere new, and the regular weekday phone calls to tell each other random things about our days, Fridays or Saturdays with *his* friends joined the rotation.

He had a lot of friends. Some of them shared the same last names but were not related. I tried to keep track by adding a memorable factoid to the nickname. Annie Yoga Instructor. Calvin Vegan. Luigi Restaurant Owner. Paulie Struggling Actor. If it wasn't so exhausting, I'd try to get to know each and every one of them. Surely they would be fascinating in some way. But I held back, and even after hours sitting at a table having drinks together, I never really bonded with any of them.

I tried to analyze why.

Reason number one: I lacked the social skills. This was an entire bundle of issues, from my lack of fashion flair to the way I had to take a deep breath and walk into a room of strangers like I was preparing for a ride on a roller coaster. It didn't help that every single friend I was introduced to said, "*So this is her?*" or might as well have said it. Anton's girlfriend! She exists! What a novelty.

They were probably thinking how long I'd last. Strangely, Anton didn't seem to notice.

Reason number two: Maybe I was too young and sheltered. Or too polite. There was something about the way the conversations went with his crowd. Smart, but sometimes nasty. I may have offended some friends because of frank opinions, but at least I said it to their faces. My parents didn't raise me to talk that way about other people when they weren't in the room, so I shut up.

If that made them think I had no opinions, I told myself that it was better than anyone mistaking me for being ill-mannered.

Reason number 3: Maybe I wasn't pretty enough. And I didn't mean super thin, model-tall and made of porcelain—I didn't *act* like a pretty person. Not the way Andrea, Anton, Charlie, Kat, and everyone else who'd come to accept that they were attractive and could use it for personal gain did. The things that happened to me at work, the fact that I was never really anyone's object of desire, that I "grew" on people—these things wouldn't have happened to the pretty.

"I need to borrow something," I said, barging into Andrea's room but stopping short at her open closet.

When we were younger, her clothes were off limits to me, but now she considered it an acknowledgement of her good taste when I borrowed anything. She directed me toward a new dress and hesitated for a second.

"I don't think that'll fit me," I said.

"It's not that... I've never worn it. It's weird that I'm letting someone else wear it first." Then she smiled. "Whatever. It's for a good cause."

***

Friday night drinks were at a bar in Quezon City with Julius Fitness Instructor, Mark World Traveler, Mark Bar Owner, and—not kidding—Marc Hotel Sous Chef.

Anton did a double take when he saw me in Andrea's dress. The good kind of double take. And it relieved about five percent of my discomfort at wearing it. The straps, for one, were too thin, so I had to wear a strapless bra for only like the third time in my life, and maybe it didn't fit right because I kept worrying that gravity would notice and pull it down to my waist.

"Is that new?" he asked.

"Yes, but not mine."

"You look great."

He did too, as always. It felt redundant to even say it aloud. It took an expensive dress to clean me up nicely, yet he was just in what was essentially a white shirt with a collar and dark jeans.

Only Marc Hotel Sous Chef had another date with him. I didn't even get her name, but when she spoke, she had an accent that reminded me of Christy's, and I noted that though she looked Filipino, she probably didn't grow up here. She was sitting on the other side of the U-shaped booth from me, and there was a band I didn't recognize playing original rock songs I didn't know, so I couldn't follow up the introduction anyway.

The place was loud, but at least there wasn't much pressure to speak.

The table was dominated by male conversation anyway. Mostly about the gym, since they all went to the same one, and other kinds of training they could do or check out. At least, that's what I gathered between songs.

This particular crowd didn't bother to include the dates in the conversation at all. Girl With Accent and I were all but invisible except to our boyfriends, speaking up only to order another drink. I felt like I should mind, but nah, I didn't—too much effort.

I needed to go to the bathroom. It was by the kitchen, unisex, and occupied. I stood in line for it, and noticed that Mark World Traveler lined up behind me.

"So I heard that Anton's met your parents," he said, the first thing he ever said to me apart from repeating my name earlier when we shook hands.

"Yeah," I said. "He's at the house almost every week."

"That's amazing," Mark said, laughing. "Never thought Anton would go traditional for anybody."

It sounded like it should be flattering, but not. I couldn't tell. "I don't know what to tell you. He's been a gentleman."

"I'm shocked. I guess people can change."

"What are you talking about?"

"Well, you must have thought about it, Julie. It's Julie, right?"

"Yes it is."

"You must have heard about what our boy was like, just a few months ago."

I shrugged, trying to be nonchalant. "I've heard things."

"And then, overnight, he's not that guy anymore. Now he's suddenly the kind you'd bring home to your parents. Know what I mean?"

"I know what you mean."

"So you don't think that kind of guy is a ticking time bomb?"

"What do you think?"

Mark had a hint of a sneer on his face. "It doesn't matter what *I* think."

"Anton and I are fine."

"I'm sure you are. Just saying—that guy is *good.* He'd be going out with two or three girls at a time in the same month, and they wouldn't know about each other. And even if they found out, he would be, *'So what?'* They all knew what they were getting into. But I'm sure he's totally honest with you."

What kind of friend was this guy? I wasn't sure if it was because I didn't know him, or the noise, or the cocktails I'd had. I couldn't figure out how I was supposed to react to this, if he was making fun of me, if I should laugh it off or what.

Suddenly it was my turn at the bathroom and I excused myself. And promptly renamed him Mark the Asshole.

Chapter 10

Why was I even annoyed? I *knew* all of that. Duh, I thought of all of it already, even before Mark the Asshole managed to say it to my face. Why else did I only agree to go out with Anton in neutral territory?

"How do you know someone's cheating on you?" I asked my sister.

Believe me, I didn't want my main source of relationship wisdom to be my younger, flightier sister. But by then I had no choice. I hadn't confided in my other friends about him in so long, and didn't feel like dumping ten months' worth of issues onto someone.

Plus, I couldn't think of any friend who would be sympathetic toward me over this. I knew that the answer was obvious. *Once a womanizer, always a womanizer. Cut your losses now before you get hurt, or before you get married.*

Hopefully, Andrea would have something better to say than my own alter ego.

"You ask him," she said matter-of-factly.

Not the answer I was looking for. "How else?"

"Oh, I don't know. There's a bunch of different things. Weird phone calls, being unavailable for stuff, canceling on you. What clues have you picked up?"

I shook my head. "Nothing. I don't get that vibe from him at all."

"Then why did you ask?"

"Just paranoid," I said.

***

Anton lived in his own apartment, near where he worked. He had apparently lived alone since he was in college, which was something I had never really experienced. It wasn't fair to say that *I* was the typical case and he wasn't, because I knew a lot of people who had to live in dorms when they went to college. I noticed that his family wasn't as much a part of his daily life as mine was. At times he'd mention he hadn't seen his parents in months, and that to me was unthinkable.

We were having dessert one Sunday night at a small café along Katipunan and I asked him why I hadn't met his parents yet.

I didn't know what I was expecting—a flash of guilt maybe? But it wasn't there.

"Do you want to?" he asked.

"I feel like I should," I said. "I mean, my parents see you all the time."

"Okay," he said. "I think they'll be back in the country by Christmas. We can set it up."

"They're not here?"

"Retired. Trying out life in the US right now. I bet they'll be back when it starts to get cold."

"Oh."

This exchange wasn't satisfying; it felt like I tried to take a big step and stubbed my toe on something. Rather than leave it at that, I took another step.

"How many exes do you have exactly?" I asked.

Anton wasn't looking at me right at that moment. He had his arm raised, reminding the waiter of the two cups of coffee we had ordered that hadn't arrived yet. When he faced me, he chewed on the inside of his lip before speaking. "I thought you didn't want to talk about this."

I didn't. I mean, I had an idea what his life was like, but agreed to give him a fair chance. But it was dumb of me to be completely unaware of his history, right? This was the smarter thing to do.

"I've only had one actual girlfriend before you," he answered.

"What happened?"

"I don't know. It wasn't as fun as I thought it would be. We lasted three months and decided it wasn't for us. We were too young, and everyone made it out to be so serious."

"How old were you?"

"Twenty? Twenty-one? It was right after college."

At twenty or twenty-one, I *had* been psyching myself up for a serious relationship, and all I got was a date here and there.

He was thirty by now, I remembered. "So everyone else...?"

"Not girlfriends."

"How many?"

This made him uncomfortable, but probably because he knew it would make *me* uncomfortable. "I don't know."

"You don't know."

He shrugged. "I wish I could say something different. I really don't know."

"You can't give me a ballpark figure?"

"Maybe it's not as large as you think."

He knew that I had never had a boyfriend. He knew that as far as dates was concerned, I hadn't even been on a dozen, and some of them were repeat performances with the same guy. "It's more than twelve?" I asked.

"Okay, it's probably larger."

Mark the Asshole's line about him juggling two or three in the same month bounced around in my head, and I made a quick computation in my mind, which I then regretted and attributed to bad mental math. The number was too high.

"What are you thinking?" Anton withdrew his hand from mine. "Does it bother you? I told you—I don't have any excuses for how I used to be, but you have to judge me on something real. Like how I am with you now."

"I remember."

"Does it bother you?"

"Do you want to go somewhere?" I said instead. "Like, out of town." By no means did this change of topic mean I answered his question. I *was* bothered, but I wasn't ready to admit it yet. He hadn't done anything that would lead me to think that he hadn't lived up to my idea of boyfriend perfection.

Maybe he took it as a good sign. Then he shook his head. "Don't steal my thunder."

"What?"

"I was going to surprise you with a trip to Tagaytay on your birthday weekend."

"Oh." And now I felt like I stubbed my toe on the other foot. "Thank you. Wow. I... I'd really like that."

The waiter brought over our coffee order, and Anton unceremoniously picked up a sachet of brown sugar and emptied half of it into my cup—the way I liked it. "Is something up?" he asked. "Work bothering you again?"

Only when he said it did it occur to me that I hadn't worried about work in a while. But that was the problem with the idle mind, it found other things to make you crazy.

I pushed the thought down, down, down and buried it under cherry chocolate cake.

Chapter 11

I didn't figure twenty-six to be an exciting age. It didn't seem like a landmark year, that last year of hanging on to your mid-twenties, but not really.

I spent my birthday weekend in a lovely little hotel in Tagaytay, with a view of Taal Volcano and Lake, with my boyfriend. We had a nice, early dinner at an Italian restaurant, bought desserts and fruit from one of the roadside stands, and spent the rest of the night in our room.

There's a hazy quality to my memory of that day now, like it was shot soft-focus and artsy, showing only the folds in the sheets and hair strewn against pillows. It's like that because apparently, that was the extent of my romantic fantasies—big bed, fluffy pillows, clean soft sheets, lazing around with a loved one, eating fruit and chocolate and pie. When I rolled onto my stomach to reach for another bonbon, I saw Anton looking at me. He fit the part of the guy in my fantasy—dark skin and muscle, a hard and definite shape against the sheets and pillows. And best of all, he was looking at me with a tenderness that I wished for but never really expected to get.

I reached over and poked his shoulder with my finger, testing if he was real. The arm tensed but barely moved.

"What?" he asked.

"Just checking."

He crawled over to my side of the big bed and kissed me. He always started off light as a feather, and as I kissed him back, I would wonder who made contact first. Maybe it was his way of letting me think I was setting the pace, again. His fingers lingered on the buttons of my top, passing over them once, twice, and then I paused to handle the first button myself.

That was all he needed.

***

Sometime in the middle of the night, I put my clothes back on. Because it was cold. My boyfriend, already in deep sleep, didn't feel it at all. He was still naked, sprawled on his stomach, blanket barely covering him. I pulled it further up to his neck and sat there, hugging a pillow.

Depending on how you counted, Anton and I had been seeing each other for eleven months. It was the first time we had sex. It was the first time *I* had sex. I imagined that the experience was new for him too; it probably had been a while before he had needed to take things excruciatingly slow. I tried to get myself into it but my fantasies didn't actually *include* the, er, de-hymenization part. Which was slightly awkward, slightly embarrassing, and near the end, was almost sort of kind of pleasurable but I wasn't entirely sure, because by then he had been holding back too long and finally let himself go. Later, he reassured me that it would get better, and asked if I wanted another go, but I said it felt great and he should go to sleep.

This can't be it. Too many people—boyfriend included—were too into sex for it to be the non-event that my first time was.

Maybe it was me. I made a big deal about being ready for this only if he swore he had always done it protected, and he'd gotten the tests that were supposed to reassure me. But it wasn't that. In terms of first dates, I was probably his worst too. Maybe I was doomed to never get anything right the first time.

I looked at him, sleeping contentedly beside me. If I were him, I would have lost patience with me a long time ago. Surely he had at some point met a girl who didn't have to make him wait, didn't keep him from his friends, and no doubt was better at *this* than me.

Did he lose a bet or something? What was he trying to prove by staying with me?

***

When I woke up, there was a bright glare that beamed right into my eye.

I thought it was the sun, but wait—it was the sun's light reflecting on *a diamond ring in front of my face.*

"What?" My thoughts were as tangled as my morning hair. I fell asleep thinking more about how wrong we were for each other, and that led to dreams of breaking up, of explaining to him why we had to break up, of finding out that *he* wanted to break up and being so relieved.

But now in waking reality, I was faced with an Anton who was definitely lucid, shower-fresh, and earnestly on his knee on the carpeted floor.

"Good morning," he said.

"I'm confused."

"Let me talk first?"

I bit my lip to shut my mouth.

"I think that the past year we've been getting to know each other has been the best year of my life. I feel like I'm a better person because of you. You... you're exactly the kind of person I want to spend my life with."

I searched his face for some kind of tell, but I did know him quite well by now, and he actually did believe what he was saying.

"Are you serious?" I asked.

"I finally am," Anton said. "You're strong, you've got your own mind, you're so grounded, you're beautiful... Julie, will you marry me?"

The fantasy may have included this, but instead of shrieking yes, I said, calmly, "Why?"

He blinked.

By the end of that day, I was not engaged and I no longer had a boyfriend.

Chapter 12

Seven months later

Harry was wearing the dark green shirt with the starched collar. Again.

Harry Panganiban joined my place of work about three months ago. Didn't work on my team, and I forgot how we met exactly, but we'd been having lunch nearly every day since mid-March.

It wasn't as weird as I thought it would be. I *did* have friends, you know, before. And I was entirely capable of making new friends. Plus, Harry wasn't bad to look at. In fact, he was objectively quite handsome. Nice skin, symmetrical features, slightly scruffy the way guys who were unaware they were good-looking tended to be. He'd probably look better after some fashion advice, but I wasn't in any position to give him any. He wouldn't have known what to do with it if he got it anyway—I complimented his dark green shirt once and since then, he started wearing it more often.

"Have you read it yet?" he asked, as he usually did.

"Sorry, no," I answered, as I usually did. "This weekend, I promise."

Harry liked to lend me books and DVDs of things I "absolutely must see." That led to a pile of unread books and unseen boxed sets growing on my nightstand. It wasn't that I didn't want to entertain myself with these things, or that I felt like I wouldn't like them. But I was in *rut mode* and was in no mood to do anything.

This was in stark contrast to the first three months after I broke up with my first serious boyfriend. Back then, I was a hyper bunny, bouncing from new purchase (fancy digital SLR camera) to new hobby class (pottery) to new fitness trend (belly dancing). And then I got really tired and quit all of them.

Since then, my life picked up exactly where it had left off pre-Anton. Spent weekends at home. Spent weekdays at work. And did nothing much. Agreeing to have lunch with then-new employee Harry was a small step in *a* direction, not exactly sure whether it was a right or wrong one.

Harry was a writer too, but for a different team at work. Something about it made us instantly gel as friends, a camaraderie over shared experience. He was new to the office but had enough talent to possibly be an editor soon. He, too, liked to read, spoke well, and—probably the most impressive thing I noted about him—was as comfortable writing in Filipino as he did in English. My secret shame is that I cannot string together a kickass paragraph in my native language. He could, and it was too bad he was employed at our so-called "global workplace" where this talent was of no use.

We ordered food. He went with classic beef *tapa* with the fried rice and egg. I chose pork *tocino*, because since my rut started, I had no strength to guide myself toward healthy food and instead chose what looked satisfyingly oily.

This was how a *manang* self-destructed, probably. Not with drugs or alcohol, but cholesterol.

"...so what do you think? What should I do?"

"What?" I said, snapping out of one of those trances I tended to slip into.

Harry was getting used to it. "The mistake I found. Do I tell Marge about it, or let Christian handle it?"

One of the signs that Harry was on his way to an editor track was his concern over the work that other writer teammates put in. He would identify errors in their work, but wasn't sure whether it was crossing the line to point it out to an equal.

"I don't know, Harry..."

"What would *you* do?"

"I would tell my teammate before she submits it to my editor."

"Then I'll do that."

"But my officemates hate me, so maybe you *shouldn't* be doing things they way I would."

He shook his head. "They don't hate you," he said. "I would have heard something if they did."

"They don't talk about their hate *as much* anymore," I qualified my earlier statement. "Because I made it difficult for them to keep their jobs and trash talk me daily. But that doesn't mean they love me."

"I'll try it your way and tell you what happens."

"Your choice," I said. "And then watch as the sheep attack you."

He laughed, like it was the most amusing thing ever. Maybe it was because I outranked him at work, but he had a way of making me feel like the things I said were so smart and witty.

I used to protest and tease him about giving me too much credit, but even that I got tired of. So he thought I was more intelligent that the average Jane—why did I have to ruin that? Eventually, I said nothing.

Soon, our hour was almost up. We paid for our food and made our way back to our building. Lunches were often like this, simple and comfortable.

On the way back, he finally said something different: "Are you doing anything Friday night?"

I wasn't in my trance, but stalled anyway. "What?"

"Friday night. I have a late deadline and need dinner company."

"Um, okay."
"Great."

***

Seven months. That was more than enough time to finally go out to dinner with someone else; I knew that. Besides, it wasn't like I wasn't ready. Harry had been prepping me for weeks.

The other thing that we talked about when we went out to lunch? Relationships.

First, he asked me if I had recently been in one. At that point I was weak. I hadn't confided about the breakup to *anyone*. My family knew that it was over but I didn't tell them about the proposal. How could I tell them? My *lola* would be first in line to tell me how stupid I was. By then my friends knew I'd had a boyfriend, but I hadn't told anyone the full story. So when a semi-stranger gently prodded, I may have said a little more than I should.

I told him that I just came out of a bad breakup. That my ex-boyfriend was a "reformed" player-type, and that I ended it before I became another one of his girls. Strange how many of the facts were the same, but the story sounded so different. All about the spin.

Harry picked up on that quickly, and wasted no time telling me stories about friends of his who had been dumped—no, *ruined*—by exactly that type of guy.

I let him tell me these stories. There was one about the friend who was a long-time girlfriend of a professional ball player, who had to bear with groupies and denials of cheating, despite the evidence. Harry, along with their other friends from college, nearly boycotted her wedding but she pleaded with them to pretend nothing was wrong and not ruin her day.

There was the other friend who was the on-and-off-again girlfriend of her college sweetheart, and persisted in this role despite his moving on to other relationships and eventually marrying some girl he had knocked up.

This particular topic got Harry riled up. "I don't get it. He's obviously the wrong kind of guy. Why do girls still fall for that?"

The unsaid part of that was, of course—*I'm a nice guy, and I'm not like that at all.* Harry was definitely one of those "nice guys." Sure I only got info from him, but I could tell that the way he approached women was fundamentally different. He befriended them first.

I was used to that tactic. Recognized it the first time he brought up my ex. Since I was a non-threatening friend-type, the guys who usually asked me out started as friends, and then as lunch companions, and then maybe later as dinner and movie dates. This was a slow journey that could take months or even years, but guys like Harry liked to tread carefully.

"Why do girls still fall for that?" was a test. How I answered this would signal if he would proceed further or dismiss me as hopelessly pining for the wrong kind of guy.

"Your friend is thinking he'll change for her," I said once, I think after he told me the story about the sports guy's wife. "But these guys rarely ever do." I decided that to Harry, I would be the enlightened female, duped once, but got out before I was deceived further.

"That's stupid," Harry said to that. "People don't really change."

And this was why I continued to have lunch with Harry. He said things like that, things that made me feel better about the choice I made.

***

"Can I borrow something for Friday?"

Andrea looked at me suspiciously, but stepped aside so I could look in her closet anyway. "A date?"

"Maybe."

"Do I know this person?"

"Sort of. He's a slightly pudgy lit geek."

My sister paused long enough to assess if I was kidding, then sighed. "All right. We were bound to return to this." Though she lacked enthusiasm, she did pick up a lovely white silky top and hand it to me.

"What are you sulking about? You said Anton and I weren't a match anyway." Andrea, my mom, my dad—they still missed him. I put the brave face on for their benefit.

"Yeah, but he was fun. *You* seemed happier."

"I'm happy now."

Andrea smiled thinly. "As happy as a zombie can be." She reached for a plastic shoebox and thrust seriously chunky blue wedges toward me. "Enjoy your date with the lit geek."

Chapter 13

Harry wasn't kidding about having to work late. By eight PM, he had apologized for the seventieth time and said I could leave the office and hang out somewhere else if I wanted to. He didn't have to be so sorry about it; I wasn't offended or anything.

"I'll head on over to the restaurant before they give our table away," I said nonchalantly.

As I walked at a slow, leisurely pace I must have received three text message apologies from him, and after the third one, I didn't reply anymore. He was overdoing it a bit.

By the time I got to the restaurant, I managed to find a way to switch reservations with a group that had arrived early. I was asked to wait at the bar and go over the menu. The bartender asked me if I wanted anything, but I waved him away.

"Julie, right?"

The girl who took the stool beside me was pretty—and she had that accent. *Marc the Sous Chef's girlfriend.* "Yeah..."

"Natasha," she said cheerfully, and I was glad she didn't give me grief over forgetting her name. "It's been a while! Are you here with Anton?"

"Me? No. That's over."

"Oh." Her features were dainty and almost cartoon-like as she made a sad face for my benefit. "Sorry about that. Did you break up with him?"

Maybe I should have started with a drink after all. "Yes."

"Good for you then," Natasha said, and there was something about her smile, that knowing look... and then I realized why and almost slipped off my stool.

"You dated Anton?" I was glad the restaurant was noisy; maybe it hid traces of the whine in my voice.

Natasha laughed. "Of course I did, darling. That's how I met Marc!"

***

Four years ago, Natasha, communications assistant manager at an NGO, met Anton at a mixer for some cause. ("I think it was recycling, or something.") She was there for work, he was someone else's date, but of course that didn't matter.

"I think they fought that night or something," Natasha shared, but from the lack of detail I could tell that she didn't care either way. "But he started talking to me, and I was charmed. You know."

I ordered a beer.

"Light?" the bartender asked.

"Pale," I said, choosing the kind with more calories per gulp.

"He has this way of sucking you into his world, you know? I met so many people. It was fun."

That was pretty much the opposite of what my relationship was like, but I didn't tell her that.

Once the thrill of hooking up at a work thing wore off for Natasha, their other dates didn't go so well. On their last date, Marc the Hotel Sous Chef showed up, and she found a stronger connection with him.

"It's not awkward for you? Aren't they friends?"

Natasha shrugged. "They don't mind. Why should I?"

When Harry finally arrived a minute later, he was curious about my beautiful friend and wanted to know what we were chatting about. Natasha's eyes lit up when she saw him. I could practically hear her thoughts. *This might be the one! He seems more like your type than Anton ever was.*

"Bad boys," I—or maybe the alcohol—said. "And why we all seem to have had at least one in our lives."

"I think we choose guys we think will give us what we need," Natasha said. "But who really knows what she needs? Nobody I know does."

Harry wanted to hear more, but Natasha's friends had arrived, and our table was ready.

"She seems smart and level-headed," Harry observed, making sure that Natasha was not within earshot. "Why do smart women fall for guys like that? I don't get it. And not knowing what you want isn't an excuse—you make decisions about what you want every day. You can't be that unaware of yourself *every day*."

Lying was part of it. Lying to yourself and pretending not to know things.

I let him talk about how smart and empowered I actually was.

Chapter 14

My workplace didn't issue a business phone for me, but they may as well have. My mobile phone, which used to get a lot of action when Anton called me nearly every day, now got mostly work-related messages. If I received a call, it was a work emergency. Text messages that came late at night were now probably from my mother ("Do you have your key?") and other random texts in the middle of the day were probably from Andrea ("I left my _______ at home! I'm so stupid.").

So the call from Kat was unexpected, but welcome. It had been months since I had even seen her—and since the breakup, I hadn't seen her at all. On the surface, she seemed to fit right into Anton's crowd of attractive alpha-type partiers, but she only *looked* the part, if that was even possible. I found her funny, down-to-earth, and even with the handsome TV star boyfriend, she seemed like she wasn't really part of that circle. Or at least, she always acted like she would rather be talking to me.

During another Mickey and Margo dinner, back when Anton and I were together, she told me about her relationship with Charlie. I was glad she brought it up, because I wanted to ask about it. "Apollo Ortiz," you see, had a highly publicized relationship with another young actress. I knew this because Andrea was a fan and watched them hold hands and admit to their relationship on a celebrity talk show a few weeks after I met Charlie for the first time.

"So what's that about?" I asked her, relieved I finally could. "That girl was like crying on the talk show, she 'loves him so much' and all. Is that all fake?"

Kat laughed. "Oh I have no doubt that she totally believes she's in a relationship with him."

I didn't get it. Kat had to explain it to me. She and Charlie Finnegan had been sort-of together since they met in college. She wrote a student film, he starred in it. Since then, they were thrown into work situations together, him in the spotlight and her behind it.

"Do these actress girlfriends know about you?" I asked. "That you're actually *with* him? And how involved does he get with them?"

Kat smirked. "A lot of them are naïve and still guarded heavily by a stage mom. He gets the most action with them when *I* write a kiss into his show. They get all excited about it. And they eventually find out about me."

"You're sure about that? What if he's screwing all of them and lying to you about it?"

"Oh, we're not like that. It's not like he comes home late and I scream at him. I can usually tell if he's into someone else, and that's happened before. Right now, nah. It's me."

I couldn't do anything but shake my head. Kat was either amazingly enlightened, or hopelessly in denial. I gave her the benefit of the doubt and sided with the former. "That is *so* strange."

"Not for me anymore. I got used to it. For now and the next few years, this is going to be his life. It's useless for me to get annoyed by any aspect of it."

When we had this conversation, I was in the middle of my struggle to try and fit into Anton's world. Or at least try to sit there in that world quietly and survive. Kat and Charlie's strange relationship gave me hope that all I needed was to change my mindset to one of acceptance.

But then he had to go propose, and that threw me off.

Anyway—I was glad that Kat still considered me enough of a friend to suddenly call me and drag me to another Mickey and Margo party. She said that she and Charlie would be picking me up in a few hours. I told her I was still at work and that she should swing by my office instead.

I probably should have pretended that I had plans and that it was too short notice, but I did miss her company. I had every right to maintain my friendship with her.

***

Kat met me at the lobby of my building, her breath coming in short gasps.

"I promise you I didn't know that Charlie invited him too! I thought we were going to Makati to pick you up but we turned into Valero and stopped in front of his office and suddenly he's in the car I'm sorry—"

Him could only be one person.

It was entirely possible to see him again in this small world we lived in, but if he rejoined his old circles I didn't expect to see him at all. We didn't overlap.

But we would, if I made the mistake of stepping back into his space.

I felt it would be immature to back out on Kat right then. It *had* been several months.

"It's all right," I went, and I hoped Kat believed me. "We'll have a great time, eat the food. It'll be all right."

Then I got in the car and it *was* like old times: Charlie driving, Kat in the front passenger seat, and me and Antonio U. Santos in the back. Except there was no hand-holding, or hand-kissing.

In fact, Anton didn't even return my big, nice-to-see-you smile.

Chapter 15

If I were the mushy type, and if someone happened to witness my mushiness, I would have said at some point that Anton made me feel warm and loved. It's kind of horrible that I only came to terms with that after the breakup.

There was none of that warmth in the car right then. We might as well have been in Siberia.

Charlie had to make one more stop before we proceeded to dinner. We pulled over at a wine store, and my ex-boyfriend hadn't yet said a word to me. As Charlie and Kat left the car, I thought of maybe saying something safe and pleasant. But as I turned, Anton had already left, slamming the door behind him.

This wasn't how I thought it would turn out, and it was kind of puzzling.

I didn't think he would still be *mad*.

I followed him to a tall stack of cartons of Australian red wines and tapped his shoulder. "Hey." The muscle was hard, and I was surprised to feel the warmth of his skin through his shirt. He wasn't frozen, after all.

"What?" He was annoyed.

"Hello."

I noticed he checked me out. Anton's eyes had habits and he wasn't always able to control them. When he looked at a woman, he did a sweep of her body, and something in his eyes would show if he approved or not. He tried to tone it down when we were together, but I still noticed it. He had done it again to me, and he liked what he saw.

The bad habit *I* picked up was that I did the same thing to him. My eyes fixated on three key points. First was his forehead; I could see his eyes without actually staring straight into them. Next, I looked at his shoulders, from the blades and down his biceps to his elbows. If he had a long-term relationship, it was with his gym, and I found myself unconsciously checking out his progress. The last point on my sweep was his hip—whichever one was nearest me. I used to reach over and touch it...

We noticed exactly what the other did, and we both blinked a little too deliberately. He added an annoyed little frown. "I didn't know they had invited you too."

"You wouldn't have come if you knew?"

"I could be somewhere else instead, yes."

Okay, that stung. People had been mad at me before, because of things I said and did, and I could never get used to it. I always had good intentions. Why couldn't some people get past that?

"Do you want them to drive me back home?" I demanded.

"It doesn't matter. They invited you."

"What do you want me to do?"

He stepped around me, reaching for a random bottle of wine, suddenly finding it incredibly fascinating. It was as good as a dismissal, and I let him have this one. A few moments later Kat called us back to the car.

***

"I'm really really *really* sorry," Kat whispered as soon as she got me alone in Margo's house. She of course noticed that despite the ice-breaker type questions, Anton didn't say a word during the drive over. Instead, we listened to Kat and Charlie talk about work, which was fine, but didn't mask the tension at all.

"That was so *weird*, right? I'm not imagining things?" I hissed back, my mouth hidden behind my *dalandan* margarita.

People didn't like to admit it, but *I* always thought that relationships were held in place by the person who had the power. In mine and Anton's, I knew that it was him. How could it have been any other way? My last real relationship was... wait, I never really had one. I didn't count the almost-relationships with guys who acted sweet on me but didn't really stick around.

On the other hand, Anton *dated.* I didn't know as much about it then as I did now, but he had experience. He almost always initiated the breakups. I got into that relationship eyes wide open. I had enough sense to know that monogamy wasn't in his nature, and he was bound to get sick of me at some point.

So I sincerely thought that even though *I* had broken up with him, he would have seen it as liberation and eventually forgiven me. I mean, it was one thing for me to obsess about what could have been. But him? He would have recovered like a free-falling cat.

"This is not like him at all," Kat muttered that almost to herself. "Interesting."

"I know, right?"

"Well, I don't know. The whole time he was with you was *not like him at all.*"

***

The theme of dinner was "Bicol fusion" and though it was wonderfully spicy and coconut-milky and rich, I couldn't help but be distracted by the one guy at the table who would not look at me.

Was this grade school? Come on.

Margo was flirting with him the whole time too. It didn't mean that she noticed the subtext—it meant she was being Margo. But Anton didn't try to dodge her this time.

He flirted back, in that tongue-in-cheek way that couldn't be serious (because Botoxed middle-age women weren't his type, but he was a master at making someone feel attractive), but still. So he was in a flirty mood but couldn't be bothered to be civil to me?

After dinner, I found him in what Mickey called the "game room." The guys tended to hang out there because it had a pool table and the latest gaming console. Kat referred to it as the "little boys' room" but little boys' room be damned, I walked in and pulled my ex-boyfriend out of there.

I wasn't sure where to go, or how far he would let me drag him, but we got halfway up the staircase before he shook his wrist free.

"What are you doing?" he demanded.

I didn't have a speech ready. I really did think that if I saw him again all I had to prepare was the fake smile, because he'd have his arm around some supermodel and I wouldn't have to do anything else.

Next thing I knew, I was kissing him, without even checking if we were alone, pushing him against one of Margo's tall potted plants. He caught me before we caused any damage, but kissed me back anyway. It was a different kind of kiss, like it was *angry* or something.

"I miss you," I said. That was true, and also probably the most disarming thing I could think of saying.

"Nice of you to say so," Anton said, dripping with resentment and walls still up. "Since the split was your idea."

"Why are you so angry?" I hissed. "What did I do to you now?"

"Aside from wasting a year of my life? You think you should have done more, maybe robbed me, beat me up, run me over with a car?"

"Why are you mad at me? I'm sure my life has been suckier than yours since we broke up."

"Julie, I had an engagement ring designed for you and you said no."

Did I know that? I think I did and conveniently forgot about it. "Well..." I sputtered. "That's just money. I have no friends and no life. I'm sure *you* bounced back easily. My life went back to boring, only worse."

A pause. "You look hotter though."

I couldn't help but laugh. "It's probably all the weight I lost from not dating." And there it was—the hint of a smile—and my heart did a happy little skip. "See? We broke up and months later, I'm the loser. Don't be mad at me; you should be polite to me out of pity."

Anton's expression softened. He moved away from the potted plants and violated a cardinal rule in our hosts' house; he sat on one of the steps. "Why did you even do it?"

"We talked about this before—"

"I know, you talked my ear off about it. But now I want you to tell me what the real reason is."

I sighed. "You really think I wasted your time?"

"You had fun, didn't you? I treated you right, didn't I?"

Yes and yes.

"Then what the hell does '*I don't feel like I really know you*' mean? You spent a year with me. You probably know me better than most of my friends do."

Technically, I had said, "*Thank you, but I can't. I feel like I don't really know you yet.*" He was so offended. We argued over those words for a long time, until he gave up trying to understand, and I gave up making him. By the end of it all, he didn't even want to see or talk to me, much less stay in our relationship.

Now I had a new perspective, after all the stories I'd heard. I probably could make him understand this time.

By some miracle, we were still alone, so I went for it. I told him that in the past few months, I'd met a few of "his girls," Rikki, Annemarie, Mika, Natasha... At first, the names didn't sink in, but when they did, he started to look a little sick.

"Before you totally freak out," I said, "wait a second. I didn't go around looking for them, and when I met them, I didn't ask for all this info. They *gave* it to me. Because you seem to be a happy memory for most of them, in a weird way. They don't regret going out with you."

"What's your point?"

"I'm getting to that. Anton, you were a great boyfriend. But the way these girls talked about you? It was like they were talking about a totally different guy. If I told them stories about us together, they wouldn't believe me."

"I wouldn't go that far."

I shook my head. "Come on. If I tell them about when we spent Christmas with my family, and you talking to my grandfather the whole time? Or when I got sick at work?"

I must have fallen in love with him during the first incident. And after the second one, I put him on my speed dial, bumping my dad's number a few notches down.

"That's not the guy they know," I insisted. "Admit it, you were different with them."

"All right, point taken," he said. "Maybe I *was* different with you. But I was *better*. Why didn't you want that?"

"It's not better if it's an act for my benefit."

"It's not an act."

He said that so sincerely, and saying it in the present tense...

Why did I break up with him again?

Doubt probably flickered in my eyes, and he took advantage, pulling me toward him and kissing me, and it was almost like he used to. Not so angry.

"Wait," I squirmed away and struggled to focus. "Why were you different with me?"

"You still don't believe that you made me want to give up all that?"

Can someone just do that? He enjoyed dating around, living like he didn't care about anyone. I shook my head. "I don't believe it. There's something about that life you like. It's exciting. Maybe you changed for me as a challenge, but I really did think you'd go back to old habits sooner or later."

"It's not as exciting as you think it is."

Yeah right. Like I could say for sure either way. It was bad enough that he was my first real relationship, and having to hear about how exciting and spontaneous his other hookups were. None of my memories, though wonderful in their own way, would light that kind of fire. "I can't tell, can I?" I said, more bitterly than I'd intended. "I've never had that kind of relationship, and when I met the kind of guy who could give me that, he decided to *change for me*."

"Shit," Anton said as he finally got it. "I'm sorry."

"Don't apologize, please. You were wonderful to me."

"You were *bored*?"

It wasn't that...but I had paused too long that it seemed like confirmation.

He recoiled as if I had hit him, and then laughed. "I bored you to death, and that's why you broke up with me. Thanks for explaining."

"You know what I mean! It's like there's another you that these girls know, and I don't."

His hand reached up and took a lock of my hair, letting it run between his fingers. It was a thing he used to do, when he was preoccupied with something and I happened to be near him. I enjoyed it again for the entire two seconds that it happened.

Then he gave me that look. "Would you like to find out?"

"What?"

"Would you like to find out what I was like, before I met you?"

"I already know what you were like. They told me."

"No, I meant experience it firsthand. This guy you say I was."

"I don't understand—"

"Just do what I say, and you'll find out. And then you can tell me if you really feel like you don't know who I really am."

"You're crazy," I said. "I'm sure you've moved on by now. We shouldn't get back together..."

And yet the crazy idea had energized him, getting him back on his feet and pacing as he put the plan together. "But we're not getting back together, because you think I'm not capable of a serious relationship. We'll go out, hang out, that's it."

"I don't think this is a good idea."

"You just told me how pathetic your social life is. What else have you got planned?"

I winced at that. "I did go on one date with a guy."

"Who is this person?"

"Writer. Guy I work with."

"Are you going to see him again?"

"Maybe."

He dismissed the very idea of competition with a huff. "Sure, go out with him, if you want. I don't mind. But you're going to go out with me again, Julie. And if you end up rejecting me, at least—"

"I know, I know," I said. "At least it's because of something real."

He kissed me again, and it wasn't warm or loving—it was hot, and exciting, and I wasn't sure what exactly I had gotten myself into.

And I couldn't resist it.

Chapter 16

By the end of my "second date" with Harry, I suspected that there was a manual out there for dating someone like me, and he had it.

Dinner with him the last time went well enough; he probably thought that it was best to move on to step two, which was apparently lunch, on a Saturday, and then maybe a movie after "if we felt like it."

He said he would pick me up at eleven-thirty and he was there five minutes earlier. His outfit was straight from his office-casual Friday collection, and I felt for a second that I overdid it when I chose to wear a black top and a short skirt. Harry didn't seem to think so and complimented me anyway.

"You look really nice," he said. "Very fashionable."

I smiled and accepted it, like I believed him.

I felt a bit sad for my family, though. This date with Harry was by no means "too soon" but I could tell that what they were hoping would happen. I saw it when my dad left his gardening routine for a minute to check who had pulled over by our driveway. I saw it when my sister peeked from the staircase when Harry entered the house. And I saw it, the slight hesitation, when my mother accepted the box of *quezo de bola ensaymadas* from him—we were both thinking that it was from the same pastry place Anton got his from.

My fault. I may have mentioned in passing that my mother liked them; Harry, being attentive, must have picked up on it.

Lunch was at a Thai restaurant. This time, I avoided the curry, and went for bagoong rice instead. Harry asked about my family, and I gave him the highlights of our lives—jobs, ages, token trivia per person. I didn't feel at all threatened or uncomfortable as he talked to me. It was like we were at work. Except I was in nicer clothes.

"So what was your previous relationship like?" I asked him, hijacking the conversation train that seemed to consist of mostly questions about me.

Harry smiled, a little sheepishly. "I haven't had one."

I flashed back to weeks and weeks of lunches and work chats, times when he deliberately asked about Anton. I had never asked him the same thing?

"Really?" I couldn't help but make that sound teasing. "How is that possible? You're like, twenty-four by now, right?"

He retreated a tiny bit at this, but then shrugged. "All the girls I like, they like the wrong kind of guy."

"Explains the grudge."

"I sound like I have a grudge?"

I gave him a "duh" look. "Well yeah. The whole time I've known you, you've been *bad boys are baaad.*"

"It's easy to say that when each story ends the exact same way. I can't believe some people can't figure it out. Is it stupidity?"

I recoiled and tried not to show it. He still thought I wasn't one of those women. "It's denial," I said.

Since we weren't bound by the office lunch hour, we were able to eat at a leisurely pace, and even spent more time on coffee and dessert. When he asked if I wanted to watch a movie, I said I didn't mind.

He didn't try anything inside the theater—not that I was expecting him to. Even Anton saved the hand-holding for after the third date.

As we got out, my phone vibrated, still on silent mode from the move. A text: *You're going to Marc's place with me tonight.*

I replied: *Am I?*

And then: *You are. Where do I pick you up?*

Harry checked his watch, twice. “Do you want to have dinner? It’s after six and...”

This was, looking back, one of those moments. Staying with Harry and agreeing to dinner—staying with Harry period—seemed like the right thing to do.

“Actually, I need to go,” I said instead. He insisted for a bit about driving me home, but I fed him a line about needing to buy something and meet my sister who was supposedly around the corner.

Harry didn’t push it. For a goodbye, he leaned toward me and brushed our cheeks together, a friendly *beso*. A tad more intimate, but still on the side of platonic. Just like on my first date with Anton.

Maybe there *was* a manual out there.

I waved as I watched him leave, and thirty minutes later, I was in a car with my ex-boyfriend.

Chapter 17

I didn't know what to expect on this "date."

First, there was that oddly silent car ride. As soon as I got in, he nodded at me, turned up the music, and didn't speak as he drove.

"Are your parents back in town?" I said, because it felt like something a normal person would do.

He had to pause and check the rearview mirror; at least, that was how I rationalized why he replied *without even looking at me*. "We don't talk about my family."

"What?"

"You wanted this to be like the dates I had with other girls. We don't talk about my family."

"Oh. We're really going to do this?"

"*You* wanted this."

"Fine." I settled back into the passenger seat. How long before we got to Marc's place? Probably another hour, with this traffic.

I looked at my phone, and then my fingernails, and then popped open the dashboard. Copy of the registration, car manual, map of Manila, old parking receipts.

"You don't do that," he said.

This was going to be a *long* drive.

"What *can* we talk about?" I asked.

He shrugged. "Comment on the music. Ask about the car. Ask who's going to be at Marc's place."

"Who's going to be at Marc's place?"

As soon as he dropped the names, I recognized them as his friends. Charlie and Kat, the ones I actually liked, were not going to be there. That familiar discomfort started to settle in my stomach. You'd think I'd be comforted by knowing who they were, but since I never really made friends with them...

***

"You are my best *best* friend right now. Forever! Right now." I punctuated that with my third tequila shot.

Daphne Wedding Planner had been a stranger to me until an hour and a half ago but she too was in an alcohol-induced BFF high. "We're like soulmates," she gushed. "You have the *best*... opinions about my shit."

Her "shit" was a variety of boy and friend dramas, and instead of being annoyed by my instinctive reactions, she actually welcomed them. Her problems weren't new, and neither were my responses such as "*she's obviously jealous of you*" and *"he's not worth it move on please."* I didn't even remember how we started talking but suddenly there we were, squeezed together on a sofa in Marc Sous Chef's apartment, knocking back shots and sharing more than we should.

When we got to Marc's place, it was like someone flipped a switch on in my date. Anton didn't start talking to me, but he had his arm around me, and launched into some anecdote about Marc's work. I could barely hear him over the music and lively chatter, so it almost didn't even matter that he was speaking to me.

"So this is part of the demo, right?" I said instead.

"Now you're getting it," he said, into my ear, which to anyone else would have looked flirty. Then he put some pressure on the small of my back and I lurched forward slightly. "Go make friends."

"What?" I instinctively tried to grab him, keep him by my side to protect me from the sharks, but he was already gone.

Every now and then I would see him somewhere, talking to a different person, possibly flirting with other women, but my new friend Daphne was genuinely engrossing and this was better than smiling and nodding at more of his snarky friends.

"True friends don't sugarcoat," I said, toasting her glass. "Fuck sugarcoating."

"Fuck yes-men," she declared. "I don't know how it happened. All my friends are either yes-men or snakes."

"It's because you're beautiful." I didn't even hold back on that one. "It's like power. It attracts those types of people."

She paused, not sure I was serious. Then she started laughing. "Oh my God, you're fabulous. You've said what I didn't dare think. Maybe I should hook up with someone here now, just to annoy that snake."

I coughed. She giggled.

"I know, I know, not Anton, promise."

Tequila became rum cokes, and vodka sprites, not that I recalled enough to give an inventory. Wasn't even sure what else I said, but I must have said stuff, because later Daphne was giving *me* advice.

"Lighten up, woman!"

I groaned. "That's what they all say."

She somewhat drunkenly poked my face. "You have wonderful features."

"What?"

"Full lips. Cute nose. Well-defined chin. Nice proportions. In a few years, you'll find more things to hate about your face and you'll think, *why didn't I live it up when I was* whatever age you are now!"

"What do you want me to do?"

"This. Exactly what you're doing now! And don't slip back into *manang* mode—you were obviously a grouchy grouch while you were on it."

"I'm not a grouchy grouch..."

Daphne pinched one of my cheeks, forcing my mouth to pull up into a twisted smile. "Stop being grouchy, grouch! You obviously want to know where it could lead. Repeat after me: *I will not quit.*"

"I will not... quit?"

"*I will not quit until I see where this leads.*"

"I will not quit until I..."

I didn't finish, but it didn't matter because my voice was drowned out by her cheer and a drunken sisterly hug. "Yay! Go for it! I'm so proud of my best friend!"

Chapter 18

Anton's apartment smelled like coffee. It would either be a fresh, strong aroma of brewing, or flat and lingering, emanating from the several unwashed mugs accumulating in the kitchen. I didn't get the chance to give him many gifts, but on his birthday I got him a boxed set of coffee beans from all over the Philippines and he seemed genuinely excited about it.

I woke up to that familiar smell, and place, again.

If it weren't for the pounding head and slightly nauseous feeling, I would have been more panicked at that moment. I was the kind of girl who had a hard time sleeping if she didn't get to brush her teeth before bedtime, and waking up not remembering half of last night would start all sorts of worrying. But I shrugged them off and rolled out of his bed, checked my clothes (I was wearing all of them), and walked barefoot out of the bedroom. Anton lived in a two-bedroom in Makati, but the other room was a storage area. I quickly checked the couch in his small living room and it didn't look like it had been slept in.

"Good morning," he said, cheerful but not exactly warm. Like how he'd greet a colleague.

"What is that? The coffee."

"Bukidnon. Still going through that pack you gave me."

I took a seat at his small dining table. "I can't tell the difference."

"You just need to be around it enough."

It looked like he'd had his morning workout already. He was wearing shorts and a college shirt that he always had in his gym locker. He poured coffee into a mug, prepared it with the right amount of brown sugar, and placed it in front of me.

"My parents are going to *kill* me," I said.

Anton blinked like he remembered something, and picked up my phone from the top of his refrigerator. "I texted Andrea last night, pretended I was you. Asked her to cover for me. You."

"That was brilliant, thanks." Without asking, I poked into the paper bag of warm pastries in front of me, and a second later I was eating a cinnamon roll.

"My dates don't get breakfast, by the way."

I stifled a cough. "No?"

"No. Maybe coffee, but not breakfast."

"Not even *pandesal*? Offering bread is only polite."

He shrugged. "I don't really have food here in the morning. Usually."

"And you don't talk to your dates on dates either? I didn't see you *at all* last night."

"Yes."

I thought he was kidding, and paused to let him explain. He looked at me, smiling, standing by his kitchen counter sipping from his own mug. "You *don't* talk to your dates on dates?"

"Like what happened last night. I bring her along to the party and do my own thing."

"And what's she supposed to do?"

"I told you. Meet people."

That was the strangest thing I'd ever heard. "That's not a date!"

"She's not my girlfriend. I don't have to entertain her. Plus they usually appreciate that I get them to mingle. They end up meeting interesting people."

Natasha met Marc while she was dating Anton. This was probably how it happened. Hey, I *did* like Daphne. Even though I couldn't remember half of what we said to each other.

"You wouldn't happen to have Daphne's phone number, would you?"

"The girl you were drinking with? I think Marc does. You want me to get it for you?"

"Yes please." I saw the time via the display on my phone. "Shit, I have to get going."

"You can get a cab across the street from here," he said.

"So you're not driving me back to my house."

Anton shook his head and took my mug, not asking if I was done with it. "I don't do that with them."

"Fine."

I washed my face first, then grabbed my things and went for the door. He was still standing there, by the dining table, probably on his third cup of coffee by now. It was *awkward*, being watched like that. It made me feel—unfairly—that I was going on a walk of shame out of some guy's apartment.

"Bye, then, I guess." And I waved like a hyper robot, trying to be casual about it all.

Right before I closed the door, he said, "Did you have fun?"

"Yes I did," I answered. It was an automatic response, kicking in from when we were together and would go to his friends' parties. I would lie because it was easier than talking about why I didn't like his friends. But then it sank in that this time, it was true. "I mean that," I added, and then I closed the door.

What was different now?

Chapter 19

Her name, by the way, was Rhea.

I didn't ask about her, but the story—Harry's story—was volunteered by Fran and Tommy. They were a cool couple, dating for five years, Harry's friends for longer. They told me because they knew I was "different."

Rhea used to be the fourth member of this college crew. They found each other because of their similar schedules, and got to know each other better during breaks.

"We'd have lunch every day," Fran was saying. "Me, Tommy, Harry, and Rhea."

Yeah that sounds like Harry all right.

"...and most of the time, Tommy ate the same thing," Fran added.

"Best *liempo* ever," Tommy said, unapologetic.

They all hung out as friends in freshman and sophomore year, but in junior year, Harry worked up the nerve to find out if he and Rhea could ever be more than that.

This conversation made me very uncomfortable. Wasn't there a rule or something that said you weren't supposed to talk about exes on dates? This seemed like a violation of that three times over.

"What did you do?" I said anyway, because it seemed like what they wanted to hear.

Fran and Tommy both yielded to Harry, checking if he wanted to say it himself. He didn't. But they were both willing to pick up the slack.

"Harry started driving her home," Fran continued. "A few weeks before her birthday, because he wanted to ask her out then."

But he didn't just drive her home. What he did was gradually upgrade the drive to drive plus dinner, drive plus frozen yogurt, drive plus mocha latte, and finally—drive plus *three dozen roses.*

"That's a strong signal, Harry," I said. I would have whistled if I could. "I'm surprised."

He may have blushed, I wasn't sure. Fran, still into the story, was in total agreement. "It was, wasn't it? Harry had a crush on her for the longest time. He had been building up the moment for weeks. And she seemed to be really receptive."

"Three dozen roses didn't get a good reaction?" I asked.

Not at all. When Rhea was greeted by the lavish bouquets when she got home, she was shocked and not in the way he was expecting. He happened to be there because, as planned, he offered to drive her home that day for the purpose of seeing her reaction to the flowers.

"Why did you do all this? God, I'm so embarrassed," Rhea supposedly said.

He thought she knew, thought that the conversations about love and the future over yogurt and coffee had clued her in on what he was planning. Not only had she been oblivious, but she also revealed that she was seeing someone else, had been for months.

"And it was *Digs Soriano.*" The contempt in Tommy's voice surprised me.

"Ugh," Fran agreed.

"What's a Digs Soriano?"

Only the most obnoxious excuse for a college student, according to them. He had already been on his sixth year in a school where most people moved on after their fourth. Most known for his several suspensions for being drunk on campus, among other hijinks I couldn't relate to. That he was never expelled they attributed to the rich family who contributed generously to the school.

"We heard that she had gotten pregnant the year after that," Fran said. "But I never really found out, because she left school. Stopped talking to all of us."

I turned to Harry for confirmation. "You never spoke? That's how the story ends?"

"That's it, yeah," Harry said.

***

"They think you're great," he was quick to say on the drive back.

I knew that. In fact, it felt a little too much like I had dinner with his parents. They were nice, suitably impressed with my career, hopeful about my unspoken future with their friend. How was I supposed to feel, after hearing the Rhea story? I had questions I decided not to ask, like, why were they no longer friends? Because she had bad taste in men? Hadn't she been punished enough?

It was the humiliation that hurt him, I knew. He had opened himself up, and Rhea let him, without returning the favor. Surely she wasn't that dense; she could have said at any time that she had a boyfriend, but she held it back. Who knew why people did that?

Minutes later, I received a text: *Take a leave on Friday. We're going to Cebu. You'll be back Saturday night.*

"Shit," I said.

"Work?" Harry asked.

"No, it's nothing." And that was all I said to him about it.

Chapter 20

How could I say no?

I mean, all expenses paid. Airfare, bedroom at a posh resort in Mactan Island that I had heard about but never been to, buffet breakfast, possibility of the famous Cebu *lechon* at every meal.

Okay, so I wasn't there yet. Still wasn't the kind of girl who would let guys spend money on her. It was intriguing for two seconds, and then I offered to pay for half of everything.

It didn't matter to him. I had to be there, and I had to be in a separate room.

At the airport, he was dressed as if heading out to a work meeting, but without the tie.

"We're going to Mactan, right?" I squeaked, feeling suddenly silly in my shorts and yellow flip-flops.

Anton smiled, much to my relief. I didn't want to waste this day off from work because he wasn't talking to me due to twisted roleplay. "We are, but you're going to have more fun than I am."

"Oh. This is a work thing?"

"Unfortunately."

When not at parties or with strange women, Anton was quite a successful finance guy. He traveled for work several times a year, usually for conferences or training. "Not successful enough," was his retort, by the way, since he rarely got the first class treatment on these trips. He often traveled economy, and shared a room with a colleague.

"So I get my own room?"

"Yeah. I can't let you stay with Lucas and me, it's not that kind of trip," he teased.

"I get my own room but you're still bunking with your officemate?"

"Exactly."

"Why?"

He looked slightly miffed at having to explain. "Because normally, for a conference, I'd be bunking with an officemate and you would be someone who conveniently has her own room somewhere nearby. Like several floors away."

My family wasn't the vacationing type, but we *had* gone to Cebu together before. I was telling myself that so I wouldn't feel bad about spending the whole of that weekend indoors. There was so much to do! Or so much *not* to do, as it turned out. My time was my own, for once. No work—I took a vacation leave, and my boss was actually happy about that because she thought I was overworked already. No objections from the family—although I did say that I was going away with "some friends."

As soon as we arrived at the hotel on Mactan Island, Anton was whisked away by the regional conference that his office was hosting. He didn't like to talk shop, so I nicknamed the event his Annual Meeting of People with the Same Jobs. I didn't know how he could do that, by the way. As someone who routinely ranted about work, I couldn't get why one wouldn't want to do the same. Ranting about work was cathartic, at least for me. But maybe I didn't work at the right place. Maybe if I were regularly sent to places like this, to eat good food and sleep in fancy hotels for "meetings," I'd be less ranty.

***

Anton looked like he needed a drink, so I bought him one.

When I met him at the bar at midnight, I was tired. I had a long day—swimming, reading by the pool, getting a massage, enjoying the dinner buffet. It was a happy kind of tired. Drowsy and blissful.

He looked worn out. Nothing about his physical appearance betrayed it though; his shirt didn't even seem wrinkled. To the casual observer, he was just another guy, staying in the same hotel, at the bar without a date. I could have sworn that for a second I flashed back to seeing him at the gym, and the cool ease with which he carried himself in yoga class, and a shiver of anticipation broke through my drowsy bliss. But that memory wasn't mine; it was some other girl's.

Is this it? He wants me to be a casual observer?

"So, what exactly does a 'wealth manager' do?" I asked, doing my best impression of a random girl, on a lazy weekend in Cebu.

The way he smiled, it was as if I got it. "Get kicked around by rich people. What do *you* do?"

I wanted to reply with something snappy and self-deprecating, but you know what? I kind of did want to start over with him. So I played it straight. "I'm an editor."

He caught my change of tone and rode along with it. "Do you like being an editor?"

I shrugged. "I used to. I was a freelance editor before I got this job. I was a teacher, and an editor at the same time."

"That sounds like a lot of work."

"It was. And the editing jobs earned me more money than the teaching, so eventually I...became an editor full-time." I sounded sad. I smiled when I said that, but I sounded sad.

"So you don't like it anymore?"

"I used to, when I was just an editor. Now I have to work with people, writers, and they don't like me."

That was it, the simplest explanation for my misery. It was the truth, and strangely I was *not* sad when I admitted it. So many people were walking around imperfect and disliked every day, why did I let it affect me that much the past few years?

"Is it worse than being kicked around by rich people?"

I laughed. "No, probably not."

"You seem like a nice, intelligent person. I don't see why anyone wouldn't like you."

"Why do you like being kicked?"

"I don't *like* being kicked."

"Then why are you still at that job?"

He paused. "I like arguing with people I respect. I think it makes me better. I always lose, but it doesn't matter."

"That's strange," I said, only half playing now. "It's like you're into kicking *yourself* on a regular basis."

He finished off his beer in three gulps. "Do you want to get out of here?"

***

How did we end up there?

He said that the pool was heated. I said I didn't believe it. He said he was willing to bet money that it was. I said his money wasn't good enough, and dared him to jump in and tell me if a pool could keep someone warm at midnight in this weather. The next thing I knew he had taken off his shirt, emptied his pockets, and leaped into the deep end of the kidney-shaped infinity pool.

"Fuck, it's cold," he said, pulling himself up after swimming the short way to the other end.

I was cheating; I knew how cold. I *did* spend the whole day lounging around and taking lazy dips. But I was reoriented with the pool's water temperature anyway when

Anton tackled me—fully clothed in a lovely red sundress—and we splashed back in together.

When we kissed, in four and a half feet of water, lips tasting of beer and chlorine, it did almost feel like I was with a totally different person.

***

Chlorine and my hair are not friends. As it is, my hair has natural waves that can hold up against the usual Manila humidity, but a dip in chlorinated water and it becomes a brittle mess. I insisted on retreating to my room to rinse. Anton suggested that he join me.

I guess what I'm trying to say is that even though it all looks like something I wouldn't do, at the time it seemed completely logical. Compared to our first time, staged for soft-focus perfection with fluffy pillows and sheets...

Our second time, I thought, all throughout the walk back to the hotel room. *My second time*. Ever. With the same guy, except he was acting like someone else. Or himself, finally. I wasn't sure yet.

But I wasn't as nervous this time. I wanted to tell him that now, I wasn't afraid of *him*, of sex. That all the stories of his conquests filling up my head might have scared someone else but instead I was here. Curious.

He moved around my hotel room like he belonged there. Like he had been there, done this, maybe with someone else already, some other year, some other work trip. Anton shut the door, dimmed the lights, went toward the bathroom and began taking his shirt off, without a backward glance. Seconds later, I followed him in there.

Anton was facing me as I came in. His shirt and socks off, still wearing his pants. He held a small cardboard box of condoms in his hand and was working it, presumably to take one out. He looked tense, out of character. I wanted to reassure him that I wanted this. I was okay.

"Anton—"

"Julie," he said, not looking at me. It was either the most complicated box to open or the convenient excuse to not look me in the eye, just yet. "I want to tell you that—that you don't have to explain anything to me."

"Excuse me?"

He wasn't looking at me. Still the box. He succeeded in peeling the seal off it, and popped the lid open. "We broke up. If you were with anyone else after me, if you—if you feel like you need to tell me anything about your sex life, you don't have to. I'm the last person who deserves any kind of explanation, and I won't ask for it. What we do here now can just be that, what we did here."

Somehow I doubted that this was the standard opener for a one-night stand. "I don't..."

"It means," and those eyes finally found me, "that I wasn't enough for you before, and I'm going to try like hell tonight to change that, but you shouldn't—you shouldn't feel obligated to stay with me. Or do this again, if you don't want to. That's not what this is about, okay?"

I wasn't thinking that at all. Didn't I think that *I* wasn't enough for him? What a quaint concept, now that I was all ready to jump him.

So I did. No explanations necessary, for him or me. My soaked clothes joined his on the floor. My lips stayed on his mouth, kissing him liked I meant it, liked I missed it more than I could say. The water was warm but the tiles cold against my back. There in the shower, with his fingers, our mouths together, I climaxed for the first time.

Our eyes met; I saw him.

I knew the man I was with that night. And he was looking back at me, knowing instantly that it was real, how

I'd given myself completely to the experience, in a way that I never did before.

Later, when we made it to the bed, he was gentle right when he needed to be, and urgent right when I needed him to be. Our second time was making the first time a footnote. But I wasn't afraid or nervous this time. I was *ready*. I desired him. All that power, all that longing, for me. I held his head against my chest as he climaxed, feeling like I was holding him steady.

Like I knew exactly what to do.

It was cold, in my room. I remember shivering on damp sheets. And then, later, not caring, instead warming my feet by slipping them underneath his thigh and the crook of a knee.

Very early the next morning, I woke up alone, wrapped in a standard issue hotel blanket. With a vague memory of being told I was missed, and maybe loved, but he had to go.

Or maybe that was a dream.

So there I was, only in a damp blanket and the skin I was never really comfortable in, and I felt... great. And I thought of that notebook, and the entry for this weekend: Julie, editor, work conference in Cebu.

Chapter 21

In Apollo Ortiz's first movie, he played a slightly squarish yuppie who meets a free-spirited girl (they even put the actress in a pixie cut wig) and spends the rest of the movie fighting his attraction to her charming, free-spirited ways, only to succumb to them in the end. Before that, he tries to have a relationship with the "right" kind of girl—straight, dull hair, dressed in gray, reliable. But he doesn't love her, and the lesson is that a guy would not choose "reliable" over charming and flighty. Unless we're talking about cars, but even then, not always.

Andrea loved this movie because it suggested she would find that great love despite being the way she was. I wondered how that kind of girl could live with making crazy decisions all the time. Must be exhausting.

Maybe that kind of girl is fine with her decisions, because she doesn't dwell. She goes for it, owns it, and if it all goes to shit... then she picks herself up and tries not to fail the same way.

That kind of girl would not have listened to a *manang* like me, who warned people of gloom and doom based on the failures of others and not her own. I meant well, but maybe hearing all those stories made me a little too afraid of trying and being another cautionary tale.

So what kind of girl was I now?

***

As agreed, Anton and I didn't talk much about it. Not during the plane ride back, not while we were in line for the metered taxis together at Terminal 3. Instead, we talked about the flight (smooth), the airport (not that crowded for a Saturday), and swapped taxi stories (he had a drunk driver once, I had a sleepy one). When I finally got to the head of the line, he helped me with my bag.

"Did you have fun?" he asked.

"I did," I said, and again it was true. And suddenly I was in a cab, alone with my thoughts, which would have been weird except that my thoughts were warm and happy. I had to admit—I stepped into his world again for a moment and still liked it. On the ride home, I made a new personal rule: No talking.

Which was violated about twelve hours later when Andrea jumped onto my bed on Sunday morning, shaking me awake.

"Who were you with in Cebu?!" It had all the qualities of a shriek except for the volume, obviously to keep my parents from hearing.

"I'm not talking about it."

"Manang..." She grabbed me by the shoulder and continued shaking me. "Nang, you have to tell me. Who were you with?"

The way she looked at me, it was as if she knew something. What did she know? And how?

"Anton," I said, because I was too sleepy to lie.

"Holy shit." She collapsed against me in a sort of awkward bear hug. "That's not so bad. I mean, I thought it was the lit geek or some other guy."

"Why are you even asking me this?"

"I went through your bag to get the sunglasses I lent you. You don't hide your birth control very well."

Oh God. Maybe this was still a dream, one of those crazy ones, and I would wake up from it eventually. But Andrea kept talking into my ear.

"...so are you getting back together?"

"I don't know."

"What? So what about that other guy?"

"What about him?"

"So he's still around? While you're taking sexy vacations with your ex?"

I had no ready answers. This was why I came up with the No Talking rule. I tried to kick her out of my bed, but it only delayed the questioning to after lunch.

"Why did you sound relieved?" I asked her.

"Did I?"

"You were relieved when I told you it was Anton."

Maybe it was because she was my sister, but I could interpret split-second changes in her expressions. She didn't always share with me what she thought, but this time I didn't want to let it go.

"Why should I be relieved?" she squeaked, a guilty little mouse. "I mean, I know you. You had your reasons to break up with him, right? And I'm sure they make perfect sense, because you're a perfectly sensible kind of girl."

"Do you think I should get back together with him?"

"Are you still seeing the lit geek?"

"His name is..." And then I sighed. "No, I won't tell you what his name is."

"But are you still?"

"We work together. I'm going to *see* him whether I want to or not."

She shook her head, plopping down on the couch. "I'm *really* conflicted about this. Spent the whole of lunch thinking about it."

"I feel bad that my life gives you these feelings, Andrea."

My sister peeked over her shoulder, making sure the parents were out of earshot before she continued. "I don't know what to say, Nang. On one hand, I kind of want you back with Anton. He's just, you know, nice to look at. And you clicked, right?"

"Yeah."

"But on the other hand..." She paused. In fact, Andrea stopped talking altogether and started to get up from the couch.

At which point, I pinned down on one of her legs with my elbow. "What?"

"You won't hate me, right?" She yelped like an injured puppy. "But you... I don't know. Are you delaying the inevitable?"

"What's inevitable?"

"Ending up with a guy like the new pudgy lit geek."

As soon as she said it, I almost wished she didn't, because she didn't have to. The whole time with Anton I felt that *I* was the phase he would grow out of, but I didn't address what was just as possible: that he was mine. That my destiny was the other kind of guy, a guy like Harry, and I was *delaying the inevitable* by seeing Anton again.

If this was true, then I was due to hurt him again.

"I'm a horrible person," I said.

Chapter 22

This one particular story about Anton I could have gotten earlier, since I actually knew the girl personally, but part of me didn't want to hear it. I wasn't sure why. And even when I decided I was ready, I didn't call her up and ask for it. I went to get a treatment at the nail spa that I knew she visited, because that was where we bumped into each other on the day that she gave me Anton's phone number. She wasn't there on my first visit, but on the second time three days later, the universe gave me my "serendipitous" moment.

For the purposes of the notebook, she was "Carla Alejandro/admin assistant/11 years ago."

Carla was Anton's best friend, and also his first girlfriend, which I would have considered fishy had I not known for a fact that she was happily in a relationship. With one of my own friends, hence the connection. I hadn't seen her in a while, but I knew where I could go to run into her.

So there we were, sitting next to each other, getting our toenails painted.

She found it funny that I wanted to know about their time together. I could see that she and Anton had a jokey, playful friendship, and she cringed visibly when I asked her about when they were a bit more than that.

"Don't get me wrong, it's not that I have anything to hide about it," she said, "It gets hard to remember why I liked him that way back then. But I'll try. What do you want to know?"

I shrugged, as if I hadn't been thinking about this for weeks. "What was he like?"

Carla smiled. "He was sweet. I liked that he and I could talk. He also acted like a big shot, which was annoying in college, but I guess that's why he's good at his job. And he was also fatter. We both were."

"Did you think he'd become the kind of guy he... that he'd date around?"

"That he would become a slut? No, he didn't seem like the type when we were together."

"So he changed?"

"Yes, but I don't know. I mean, I know he *changed* because he lost weight and started wearing nicer clothes and had a different date every other week. But on the other hand, he didn't drop his old friends. He remembers birthdays, helps out during emergencies. He was always there for us, still is, so in some ways he's still the same guy."

"Why did you break up?"

She shrugged. "I don't know. We never really stopped feeling like friends. In a way that's great for a friendship, and bad for a relationship. We didn't even fight when we broke up. We super calmly agreed to end it."

"You didn't try to work on it, maybe there would be a spark eventually?"

"I guess we could have. But it didn't really occur to me to try. Maybe he didn't think of it either. I don't feel bad about it." Carla had her eyes closed until that point, but then she shifted slightly in her seat and peeked at me. "Why did you break up?"

"I wasn't sure if he'd stay the same guy," I admitted. "He was really great to me."

"And you're surprisingly non-judgmental. I mean, I couldn't have lasted as long as you did, knowing about his past."

"Does that make me stupid?"

"Oh, that makes him lucky." Carla reached over and patted my arm. "I think he's entirely capable of making stupid decisions, but this is what I know—he's never let me down."

I wasn't sure. This conversation wasn't exactly satisfying whatever it was that led me to start it. I kind of half expected her to say, like the others, that a relationship with him was a bad idea.

"Is that enough then? I mean, if you had a great foundation with him and it didn't work out, what hope do I have?" I asked, more to myself really.

"You and I are different," Carla answered anyway. "I mean, it's nice to think that we could all fall in love with someone that everyone thinks is right for us, but sometimes it just doesn't work out."

***

When Daphne invited me to her birthday/event supplier fair, and told me to bring a plus one, I had to think about it. The party itself was no question. The charming and shrewd Daphne had convinced a few of her favorite event suppliers (a popular wedding venue, caterer, pastry shop, cocktail bar, and band) to sponsor her birthday party and she would make sure to invite potential clients who would make it worth their investment. I would never have been able to come up with that idea, nor did I have the guts to carry it out. Naturally, I wanted to go.

She didn't say who the "plus one" should be, but I knew she was expecting me to bring Anton. And I did want to. I wanted to spend time with him again. The thought of being out with him, in his slightly irresponsible way, tickled me with its possibilities.

The lesson that could be learned from the stories of the other women in Anton's life was that being with him had to be fun. For however long it lasted.

But I didn't feel like I could bring him to a place that would probably remind him of weddings. That was too cruel, even for me.

So I invited Harry.

***

It wasn't so bad, really.

Harry and I could work out. I knew we could at least talk. At our lunches, we never ran out of anything to say. We rarely had awkward pauses. He didn't mind it when I sort of sat there, thinking. He was handsome, pleasant and intelligent, which was more than I could really expect, given that I wasn't an A-lister myself. My family wouldn't find it hard to like him. Andrea's eyes would stop rolling eventually. My *lola* would likely shrug and acknowledge the whole thing with a nod of approval, because I was not Andrea who had a line of guys wanting her attention. As a maybe-one-guy-every-few-years girl, this was good enough.

I didn't need to fear anything about our life together too, as I could see that he would adore me. I assumed this because I was doing nothing to charm him yet he kept hanging around. Never mind what Carla said. She was right about one thing: she and I were different. The past week or so was a fun diversion, but was I really that kind of girl? Could I actually live that life every day?

The status quo wasn't so bad.

This and similar thoughts were the playlist on repeat of my mind as I made my appearance at Daphne's party.

"This is a birthday?" Harry asked.

I almost doubted my own info, because when we drove up to the event pavilion, it looked dressed up for a cocktail party for over a hundred very well-dressed people. I may have understated it for Harry—and even for myself.

Daphne made sure I didn't feel out of place. She grabbed me in a big hug as soon as she saw me, and didn't bat an eyelash when I introduced Harry as my date. But I could tell by the way she tilted her head at me that she wanted the details later, in private. Already we had the telepathy thing going; maybe she *was* best friend material after all.

"You can order anything at the bar," Daphne said, continuing her quick tour. "This company specializes in quirky cocktails—pick from their list or demand a unique one for you. Dinner is in twenty minutes. And don't leave before trying the dessert bar!"

"I don't know anyone here," Harry said, still a little disoriented.

"I don't either," I said. "It's okay. We'll blend in."

"Is this normally your scene?"

"What? I don't have a *scene*."

"I feel very underdressed."

"We look fine."

"*You* look fine. I'm underdressed."

He was referring to the crowd. People like Daphne, some of them still in business suits, dropping by after work on a Friday. I wanted to tell him that these people weren't friends. Daphne invited clients and potential clients, so the social circles in the room didn't necessarily represent her crowd. Nor mine. Harry at that moment reminded me of myself, in my early days of dating Anton. He looked like... a kid. On his first day at big school. Putting up a brave front but would maybe would like to go home if given the choice.

Why had I been so resistant? It wasn't like I had to *like* these people. I had on a new dress, finally one of mine, and did seem dressed appropriately. It was flattering and pretty; normally I was off on these things.

I wanted to say this to Harry but the music was too loud, so I said, "Relax. Do you want one of those fancy drinks?"

I ended up getting the drinks myself, because when Harry found an empty table, he thought it best to reserve it for us. Sure, why not? He wasn't as curious about the cocktails, and asked to be brought a beer.

So I was deciding between the curiously-named Barcelona Bike Trail and the Cosmic Bubble when I felt the tap on my shoulder.

"So that's your guy?"

It's hard to describe exactly how I felt right then, maybe because several things were all happening to the same gut. Surprise first, and mostly guilt. But underneath that, excitement. And dread, but I wasn't sure why.

It was Anton, of course. If he had always been in the room I must have missed him when I first looked around. Daphne had conveniently *not* told me about this. Now this guy looked like he belonged with these people, regardless of what he was wearing.

"He's not my guy," I said weakly.

"Do you think the two of you look good together?"

I checked if he was angry, or mocking me, and maybe it was the lights, but he actually seemed sincere. And yet I didn't shut him down or walk away. I did feel like having this conversation, just not with Harry potentially witnessing it if he turned his head slightly to the left. It didn't seem fair.

So I picked up my drink and gestured for us to start walking—away from my date.

We cut through the crowd of people, past the mingling clients, the caterer's waiters, the dessert bar, and went out into a garden behind the pavilion. There was a sign for "Daphne's birthday" spelled out in glitter, pointing in the opposite direction. The garden smelled faintly of cigarette smoke. We had discovered the designated smoking area.

"I think we look fine together," I said. "I've gone out with guys like him before."

"I'm sure you have," Anton said. "He's the kind of guy you marry, right?"

Hence the dread.

"No," I lied.

"Because I'm the guy you fool around with but don't marry, is that it?"

I wish we'd had this conversation months ago, before I let those hookup stories get to me. Because I would definitely have said *no, you have it all wrong. It's about you, not me. I'm not the girl you end up with. I'm the girl you cheat on and leave.*

"Why would you think that?" he demanded.

Whoops, apparently I had said it out loud. "Because that's who you are, right?" I said. "I knew it was useless to try and change you."

"*Change* me? Because you think I was *that kind of guy*? You haven't known me for very long, Julie, but I can assure you I've only been me. I just decided to do things differently one day."

"I don't understand what that means."

"It means that a long time ago, I entertained the idea of being with one woman for the rest of my life because it seemed like the right time to do it, and it didn't work out. So I decided that it's not about being the right age, but meeting the right person. I never bothered to have a relationship with anyone else *but the right person*."

"That's a fancy rationalization for all the sleeping around, sir."

He raised his hands in surrender. "I've been upfront with you about everything. It's no excuse. I've always told you the truth, right? I'm not allowed to have an epiphany?"

See, I'd heard many stories about him, but nothing yet that would contradict anything he told me himself.

Maybe guys did have epiphanies.

"But you know why I'd think twice about your proposal, right? I knew you'd eventually get tired of me. I can't be sure you'd be true to any kind of vow."

"And you think polo shirt guy in there will? Because he never dated around?" Anton pointed in the general direction of Harry with disdain.

"That's not fair. He's not the kind of guy you are."

"I *am* that guy. He just doesn't have the balls to make the decisions I've made. And when I decided that I wanted to be with you, I was serious about it. But only because I thought—I *think*—you're the right person for me."

You don't do this to people. You don't go to someone who had carefully laid out the details of the next few years of her life, resigned to a certain kind of reality, and then shake her space.

"Why are you so sure? It's freaking me out," I said.

Anton got close enough and everything about him—even the way he was challenging me to believe him—was familiar. But it didn't feel at all like settling. "I just am. When I'm with you I don't feel restless."

Was the absence of wanting to flee the same as wanting to stay? Damn these guy epiphanies. "How can I be sure that I'm not just a phase for you?" I asked him.

"You can't be sure of anything. Or anyone. Not me, not polo shirt guy, or anyone else who comes after him. This is it, Julie. You have to choose."

Already I could imagine hearing this story as if it happened to a friend, and not me. I would have told her to give up the charade, as she obviously wouldn't be happy with anyone else.

It was true. And so I kissed him. And he kissed me.

And Harry walked out into the garden and saw us.

Chapter 23

For twenty minutes, my life became an Apollo Ortiz movie. It was all about timing.

Harry saw us at the worst possible moment. The kiss had been going on for a bit, no way to deny or downplay it. When I saw him, I looked caught and guilty, and I was sure that I was confirming in his mind that the guy I was kissing was the very reason why Harry and I weren't happening.

I could also see that a lifetime of losing to that kind of guy, and possibly several fancy cocktail concoctions, contributed to making Harry snap right then and there. So yeah, one second I was holding onto Anton, and the next, he was getting pushed toward the sliding glass doors, toward the two hundred people inside the pavilion.

Something crashed next to me. It was the glittery Happy Birthday sign I had backed into. Harry was yelling—because the only thing that could have made this any more embarrassing was yelling—things like "Leave her alone!" and "She wants you out of her life!" He kept pushing until Anton bounced off the glass barrier.

It was loud. I thought the glass would break, but it didn't. Instead it sounded like the kind of thing that would make Anton hurt in the morning. That was what made my ex-boyfriend get his bearings, and he braced to defend himself.

I yelled Anton's name, full of concern, as he managed to hit back hard enough to get Harry to step back and fall to one knee. The only thing my yelling accomplished was reveal who exactly I was worried about, and it was useless because he didn't need the worry. Harry looked up at me, and I wish I had seen something like disgust or anger.

He looked... well, like he lost a fight.

"Harry, what the hell did you do that for?" I said, which was probably not what this self-appointed knight was expecting.

"You told me about him," he said. "You told me..."

"I didn't tell you everything. Why do you think I would tell you everything? You had no right to do this."

I felt awful for him at the same time, I did. But I couldn't let him think he was saving me.

He pushed past me and left.

***

I rushed out to the parking lot, actually saw his car drive away, and did a little half-hearted run, hoping he would notice.

"You lost your ride," my ex-boyfriend said, smugly despite being banged up, because he couldn't help it.

"I have to apologize to him..."

"You don't owe him anything. Come on, let's go back inside."

"No, I'm going to apologize," I said, swatting his hand which had reached for me. "The poor guy..."

Where is my phone? Suddenly my bag seemed like a bottomless pit, and each time I reached in, my hand came up empty. But what was I expecting to do, call Harry while he was driving? Did I want him to be more irate than the average hothead on EDSA?

I didn't care; the appearance of trying made me feel less like a heartless person. At the same time, Anton was there, his hand on my elbow, pulling me back to his side. "He's not your boyfriend."

I put my arms around him, to reassure myself that he was okay. "You might want to get yourself checked or something."

"I didn't break anything."

"That looked bad."

"I spar at the gym all the time. This is nothing."

"I still need to apologize to him. He... he thought he was doing what was best for me."

"So now you know what it's like on the other side."

"What?"

Anton picked stray blades of grass from his shirt, unfazed as usual. "Did he think I was the guy who was bad for you? The kind of guy he should save you from? That was none of his business. You and I get to decide what happens to us."

Wait, what? I chose him in a very public and cringeworthy way, and he brings this out again?

"I happen to understand why he did it," I said. I was still me. Maybe I had made some different choices lately, but I hadn't really changed."You know what? You aren't either. My boyfriend, I mean."

I wished Daphne a happy birthday and called a cab to take me home.

Chapter 24

"...and that was the last time I talked to the both of them."

"Even if Harry works in your office?"

"Oh it's easy to find ways to avoid me. He probably joined the group of officemates who hate me."

"And Anton?"

"He leaves messages. I haven't returned them."

"You haven't talked to him at all?"

"It doesn't feel right, not before I talk to Harry..."

"Or you don't know what you're going to say to him."

"Who?"

"Anton."

Instead of answering, I sipped my milk tea. It was a long and reflective sip.

I bumped into Charlie, Apollo Ortiz himself, while in line at the popular milk tea place near my office. I was off work but had no other plans; he apparently had nothing better to do than listen to my story. I guess I considered myself more of Kat's friend, but he seemed to know everything Kat knew, as was the case with couples. He was a good enough substitute. Maybe even the better one for me to talk to right then, as only he could answer something I wanted to ask.

"I hope you don't mind if I ask, Charlie," I began, "But you... you love Kat, right?"

He was surprised by that. "Yeah I do."

"So that actress who's supposed to be your girlfriend...?"

Charlie shrugged dismissively. "For show. You haven't heard? We've 'broken up.'"

"Kat is okay with that?"

"Sometimes she enjoys it. She's a strange girl."

No, that still didn't answer my question. "I mean... why is she so confident about your love for her? Do you *do* anything specific to get her to trust you?"

Charlie's giant cup of tea was nearly empty, and his own long, reflective sip drained it all. "I guess I don't."

"Wow. That's weird."

"You wanted something useful for you?" He flashed that A-list TV star smile at me.

"Yes please."

"I'll try," he said. "Okay, how about this. I met Kat in college, before the whole acting thing. Or actually, I met her when the acting thing started. I loved her before this TV career took off, and during the height of it. I loved her even when she hated me because I was falling into a bad crowd, and thought I was attracted to other people, and lost my job. I loved her when she helped me get cleaned up and found me a second chance at work. I loved her when she was that cute junior who was always in black, and when she became the person who wrote the words I said on TV every day, and when she was the person who had me fired when I was showing up to work stoned. And I love her now."

"That's sweet," I said. "This is useful to me how?"

"What I mean is, she has played different roles in my life since I met her. And vice versa. But I still love her, always have. And based on our track record, I think I always will," Charlie admitted.

Because maybe it wasn't about history or chemistry. All this time I was wondering about someone being capable of change, when I should have noticed the faith he had in his choices.

"You give good advice, Apollo," I teased.

He laughed. "You think? I'm sure I said that in the movie I just did."

***

My office had an internal instant messaging program, and I decided to use it when I finally figured out what to say to Harry. I normally wouldn't have, but I felt that confronting him about *us* would be awkward because he never admitted to thinking of me that way. But that was part of his problem.

JulieC> You're doing it wrong.

Sixteen minutes later:

HarryP> Please explain.

JulieC> I know that you want to be friends first with the person who will be your girlfriend. Many girls want that too, and you'll say that you don't believe it because they always seem to choose someone else, but it's true.

HarryP> We've talked about this before. The girls I like have a thing for that kind of guy.

JulieC> Not necessarily. It could be because you're doing it wrong. Maybe you have to tell a girl earlier on that you like her.

HarryP> If we were meant for each other, we would know it's right.

JulieC> Via telepathy?

HarryP> I give signals.

JulieC> Do me a favor. Next time, say something. It doesn't have to be the first date. Maybe the third or fourth. Don't wait a year if you're sure. Certainty is sexy. And owning up to your attraction is sexy too, and if you do it right and you're not creepy about it, I bet she will respect you for it anyway even if she doesn't like you back.

JulieC> And it's not the end of the world if she doesn't like you back. If she's worth hanging out with, then she's a good friend to have. She might also change her mind, but there will be nothing to change if she doesn't know.

JulieC> If it doesn't work then I'm wrong, and you can keep doing what you're doing, if you think that'll lead you to the right person for you.

Twenty-two minutes later:

HarryP> You're really just giving advice, aren't you? You don't think of me that way.

JulieC> Yes and I'm sorry.

HarryP> So it's still him, then? That guy you know would hurt you eventually?

Someday, I was going to be able to talk to Harry and he would really see me as a friend and not another girl who strung him along while liking someone else. But not yet.

Nine minutes later, I decided to give him the victory:

JulieC> If you're right about that, you'll be the first to hear about it.

Chapter 25

I had to walk the talk. Certainty was sexy.

That led to my sudden Saturday morning trip, via surprisingly not horrible public transport, to Anton's family's house in a subdivision in Muntinlupa.

It led to being, for the first time, in the bedroom Anton grew up in. I was lying on his bed, and spent too long a time staring at the ceiling.

"What are you thinking?" he asked, trying to find that same spot of ceiling from his place next to me.

What did I think the house that Anton grew up in would look like? He rarely talked about his family, so I thought the house would be utilitarian and without personality, maybe a concrete box with a bed. Yet as soon as I stepped into the cozy split-level house, I immediately felt that he rightfully came from there.

From the gate to the front door to the hallway leading to the formal dining room, at least four people apologized to me. First was Anton himself at the gate, who asked me to wait a sec while he changed his shirt. At the door was his mother, who gave me a quick peck on the cheek after learning who I was, and immediately explained that she was dirty because they were unpacking. At the hallway I passed his father, a handsome man who looked exactly like Anton plus thirty-five years and gray hair, dragging an unwieldy suitcase I could probably fit into. He said, "Turn right and have a seat, Julie," as if we had met before, and I nodded and did as told. Then in the dining room, a barefoot pregnant woman who introduced herself as Anton's sister ushered me to a chair and asked if I was okay with a banana for *merienda* as there was nothing else in the kitchen.

I then felt a bit sorry myself, as it seemed to be a really bad time for them to entertain a guest. And sheepish, because my aggressive message to Anton that morning was, *I'm seeing you today whether you like it or not.*

And then I was alone, sitting obediently at the table. The wall in front of me was full of framed photos. Different sizes, different frames, most photos in color, but some in black and white. They weren't arranged in chronological order so I had to try and piece the timeline together in my head.

Amidst the wedding photos, old-school style portraits, and graduation photos, I saw bits of a life. Smiley baby, toddler in fatigues, first communion, basketball with other skinny teens, at least twenty pounds heavier in Hong Kong, awkward in a suit at some formal event. In a few frames, a more familiar version, at the sister's wedding, at a gun range.

My eye settled on what might have been the oldest photo of him there. He couldn't have been a year old, in his mother's arms, sticking his tongue out at the camera.

Something real.

"I can't believe you made it all the way out here." Anton had come up behind me, all fresh now.

"I said I was going to see you."

"I know." He smiled, and I almost forgot what I was going to say. "It sounded like you were about to punish me for something."

"I'm glad I came, though. This is a nice thing to see."

"Don't be fooled by the pictures," he said. "This is not a sentimental family."

"It makes you more... *real,"* I couldn't help saying. "It's nice seeing where you came from."

A photo of him as a chubby kid caught his eye and he walked toward it, wincing.

"I would always be eating a pint of ice cream, when I was this age," he said, shaking his head. "My parents didn't know any better."

"Are they back home for good?"

"At least until they decide where to go next. And then they'll call me to pack up all the stuff again."

He led me to his room. The path to it smelled faintly of coffee. Without asking, I lay down on his bed and stared up, trying to figure out what to say.

"Am I being stupid?" I asked him, finally speaking.

"About what? Because you never are."

"If one of my friends told me a story about dating you, I would tell her to leave you before she got hurt."

"You already did that."

"So why am I back here?"

Another pause. "Maybe you liked it."

"What did I like?"

"I don't know. We went out and I treated you just like the other girls. Why did you enjoy it?"

Because he *didn't really* treat me like the others. Maybe he tried, by changing the setting and characters at each new date. But it was still him, me, and our baggage present right there. I couldn't feel like Rikki or AnneMarie or anyone else from his past, because unlike them I *knew* he cared, and I felt it. It was always going to be different.

"I like having fun with you," I said. "It felt to me that you were having more fun, that you felt you were free to be you, and I guess it made me less worried that you were pretending."

"Do you know what made *me* paranoid?"

I shook my head.

He took my clammy hand and brought it up to his chest. "That you would disappear. That you would hear something, anything, about me, about something I did, and find it so despicable that you'd leave without telling me. I didn't mind it when you didn't want to hang out with my friends. I was sure one of them would say something stupid."

How strange. Hearing this, I found it silly and valid at the same time. I remembered Mark the Asshole. "Someone did."

"But then I thought, I couldn't hide forever. It was too easy to dig up all my dirt. If you found out and you ended up hating me, I was going to have to deal with it."

"I didn't hate you," I admitted. "Even after hearing all those stories about you."

"I could tell," he said. "Why do you think I had the guts to try again?"

I was glad that he was the kind of guy who did that. I wanted to be the kind of girl who wouldn't be haunted by someone else's past. Who would embrace happiness already present. Who wouldn't be afraid of an unlikely future.

Who will I choose to love, regardless?

That day, I chose him.

Epilogue

One year later

Georgia Santamaria, younger sister of the bride, wasn't sure what just happened, but she sure hoped she was witnessing the beginning of a love story. That would be cool.

Her sister Kat's wedding—to superlongtime boyfriend Charlie—was an intimate gathering at a lovely island off Coron in Palawan. It was a stressful but fulfilling weekend for the eighty guests who showed up. Everyone was probably as surprised as she was that this wedding was happening at all. Surprised but maybe a bit relieved that those two decided to make it legal.

Georgia shared a table with Kat's friend Julie, an editor. Kat made sure to introduce them because Georgia, a college junior, was thinking about a career in that herself. Julie was very encouraging. Not so excited about the career, but encouraging. By the end of the wedding reception, held on the beach, Georgia had scored herself an internship at Julie's office, and soon would be working with Julie herself.

"How do you know my sister?" she asked her new boss/friend.

"Common friends," Julie said. "We hang out sometimes."

"You're probably the least weird of her friends. You seem pretty normal to me," Georgia had to say, and she meant it as a compliment. Julie seemed... grounded. Put together. Reminded her of a teacher, for some reason.

"I actually *was* a teacher," Julie said. "Not all of my students were as concerned about their internships as you."

Georgia wanted to ask her more about that, but suddenly both she and Julie got pulled out of their seats by the wedding planner and her assistant. Then she saw herself at the center of the patch of sand designated as the stage/dance floor, with a dozen other guests. Julie was as confused as she was.

The wedding reception's host, one of Georgia's cousins, cleared it all up for them: "Thanks for volunteering to participate in the bouquet toss, single friends and family of Kat!"

Julie rolled her eyes then, and Georgia decided that they just might get along. Bouquet tosses at weddings for the single girls? So lame. She was surprised Kat allowed this to be part of her wedding.

Georgia's cousin the host continued, a tad more gleeful than necessary. "Everyone knows how this goes, right? Kat's going to throw her bouquet, and whoever catches it is next to be married. Where are the blindfolds?"

"What?" Georgia squealed, protesting as one of the wedding planners tried to put a pale blue blindfold over her eyes.

"To make things interesting," her cousin said. "All the ladies will wear blindfolds."

So I find out I've caught the bouquet once it's landed on my head? Georgia wondered, shooting a look at her sister before letting some girl tie the blindfold on her. The host counted down from three, and based on the cheers of the guests, it looked like someone managed to have a bouquet thrown at her head. It definitely wasn't Georgia.

She peeled her blindfold off and headed to her seat, but Julie wasn't with her. Because Julie was still out there, blindfolded, on the sand, with the bouquet. Georgia felt a tiny bit sorry for her, and then chose that moment to head over to the buffet table and get more dessert.

They pulled the same trick for the guys, and when Georgia got back to her seat, she saw that the groom *didn't* throw the garter out to the dozen or so guys standing there. He pretty much handed it to this one tall, really handsome guy, and that was that. None of the other single guys raised an objection, but they were blindfolded anyway, like she had been.

"So," her cousin the host said, "We're all about tradition today, right? You know what to do with the garter?"

This kind of thing was annoying if you were a single girl at a wedding, but maybe Julie would disagree just this once. Because the guy was *hot*. Like, model hot. Or professional athlete hot. In fact, they looked good together. When they were asked to take their blindfolds off, and see each other, and let the realization that they were going to have to kiss in front of strangers sink in, they still looked good together. Not that Julie seemed to be the type who'd be hanging out with guys like him. Julie smiled shyly at the guy, or maybe it was at all of the other people watching. The guy wasn't at all shy, and sort of raised a hand in a salute to groom Charlie.

As she ate more pineapple upside down cake, Georgia watched as the guy slipped the little lacey garter up Julie's leg, as the crowd cheered on. She had to hand it to Julie—she did *not* look embarrassed at all by this. It might have even been a little fun for her. The guests teased him to take it further, and he played to the crowd, asking for her permission before moving his fingers lightly, higher up her bare leg.

All the same, Georgia did *not* yell "Kiss! Kiss!" with the rest of the guests. Her dad was cheering especially loudly. Would her family *really* encourage someone to kiss some guy who caught the garter at Kat's wedding? They had to be really drunk to think this was fun.

And then the guy took her in his arms, dipped her slightly, and they kissed. It was a real scorcher of a kiss, deep and passionate, not like the token light pecks by the bouquet girl and garter guy that Georgia had seen at other weddings. She almost choked on her cake but she couldn't stop looking. The crowd first cheered for them, and then sort of quieted down when they noticed that they were still at it without their encouragement. It almost got awkward, but then Charlie took the microphone and thanked them for the entertainment.

When Julie returned to their table, cheeks flushed from all of that, Georgia flashed her a smile. "So what was that about?"

"We know each other, don't worry. Anton's my boyfriend." Julie quickly gulped down some water and pressed a tissue to her forehead. "We just like having fun at potentially boring events."

"Okay, so maybe you're not my sister's most normal friend," Georgia said.

The End

Author's Note

This edition of *That Kind of Guy* has a new cover and an extended scene.

It is still dedicated to Ula, because she helped me come up with the title one day on Twitter, and it was/is perfect.

Julie and Anton have since appeared in more of my books, such as What You Wanted, its short story Wedding Night Stand, and Better At Weddings Than You. They lived happily ever after.

Thank you, Ines, original editor of this book. It's better because she pushed me to "go there."

Thank you to Rachel Coates and Jef Flores, who read a scene from this book at a #romanceclass event and gave the characters new life. I loved their performance so much that they now grace the cover of this edition.

Thank you, readers and friends, especially the ones who keep asking me for copies of this. Here you go! Let's celebrate!

Mina

Chic Manila series by Mina V. Esguerra

Contemporary romances set in the Philippines. Can be read as standalones.

My Imaginary Ex (#1), Jasmine and Zack
Fairy Tale Fail (#2), Lucas and Ellie
No Strings Attached (#3), Carla and Dante
Love Your Frenemies (#4), Kimmy and Manolo
That Kind of Guy (#5), Julie and Anton
Welcome to Envy Park (#6), Moira and Ethan
Wedding Night Stand: A short story (#6.5), Andrea and Damon
What You Wanted (#7), Andrea and Damon
Iris After the Incident (#8), Iris and Gio
Better At Weddings Than You (#9), Daphne and Aaron

About the Author

Mina V. Esguerra writes contemporary romance, young adult, and new adult novellas. Visit her website minavesguerra.com for more about her books, talks, and events.

When not writing romance, she is president of communications firm Bronze Age Media, development communication consultant, indie publisher, professional editor, wife, and mother. She created the workshop series "Author at Once" for writers and publishers, and #romanceclass for aspiring romance writers. Her young adult/fantasy trilogy Interim Goddess of Love is a college love story featuring gods from Philippine mythology. Her contemporary romance novellas won the Filipino Readers' Choice awards for Chick Lit in 2012 (Fairy Tale Fail) and 2013 (That Kind of Guy).

She has a bachelor's degree in Communication and a master's degree in Development Communication.

Addison Hill series: Falling Hard | Fallen Again | Learning to Fall

Breathe Rockstar Romance series: Playing Autumn | Tempting Victoria | Kissing Day (short story)

Chic Manila series: My Imaginary Ex | Fairy Tale Fail | No Strings Attached | Love Your Frenemies | That Kind of Guy | Welcome to Envy Park | Wedding Night Stand (short story) | What You Wanted | Iris After the Incident | Better At Weddings Than You

Scambitious series: Young and Scambitious | Properly Scandalous | Shiny and Shameless | Greedy and Gullible

Interim Goddess of Love series: Interim Goddess of Love | Queen of the Clueless | Icon of the Indecisive | Gifted Little Creatures (short story) | Freshman Girl and Junior Guy (short story)

The Future Chosen

Anthology contributions: Say That Things Change (New Adult Quick Reads 1) | Kids These Days: Stories from Luna East Arts Academy Volume 1 | Sola Musica: Love Notes from a Festival | Make My Wish Come True

romanceclass

Made in the USA
Middletown, DE
09 November 2019

78315214R00076